CAT AND MOUSE

Fear clutched Evelyn's heart. The cat could see in the dark and she couldn't. It would catch up and spring on her. She ran another dozen strides and stopped and spun. Better to face it, she reasoned, than have it take her from behind. She never heard a sound yet suddenly there it was, a darker black than the night itself, its eyes glinting in the starlight. Evelyn swallowed and brought the Hawken up just as the mountain lion sprang. She had no time to cock it. A heavy blow to her left shoulder spun her halfway around and pain spiked her body clear down to her toes. A raking forepaw had slashed her. She turned to confront the beast but the mountain lion hadn't stopped.

It was after Bright Rainbow.

WILDERNESS #64:
DEVIL MOON

David
Thompson

LEISURE BOOKS NEW YORK CITY

Dedicated to Judy, Joshua and Shane.
And to Beatrice Bean, with the most loving regard.

A LEISURE BOOK®

June 2010

Published by

Dorchester Publishing Co., Inc.
200 Madison Avenue
New York, NY 10016

ISBN 10: 0-8439-6264-X
ISBN 13: 978-0-8439-6264-2
E-ISBN: 978-1-4285-0882-8

The name "Leisure Books" and the stylized "L" with design are trademarks of Dorchester Publishing Co., Inc.

Printed in the United States of America.

10 9 8 7 6 5 4 3 2 1

Visit us online at www.dorchesterpub.com.

WILDERNESS #64:
DEVIL MOON

Part One

The Call of the Savage

Chapter One

The moon was a white crescent in a sea of stars when the female left the ledge and came down the slope of boulders to the aspens. She was swollen and slow from the new life inside her, the same life that compelled her to hunt more often than she normally would.

The leaves of the aspens trembled in the slight breeze, their slim boles a silvery hue. She glided with her body low to the ground and her ears pricked. It was her nose that told her deer were in the meadow, and her belly growled with need.

She was more golden than tawny. Her mother had been golden, too; her father a great copper slayer who held sway over twice as much area as most males and was brought low in a clash with a grizzly. Her mother died when she was but a winter old, taken by a pack of starving wolves in the deep snow when she could not move as fast. Her mother had been defending her and her brothers and a sister, all of whom had long since scattered to live lives of their own.

That was the nature of their life in the wild. A life that was hard and brutal. There were the quick and there were the dead, and for eight winters now she had been quick enough to go on living and to give birth to two litters besides the young now taking form.

She was in her prime, all sinew and muscle. She was bigger than most females, but then her line was nearly always bigger. She did not know why that was.

She came to the last of the aspens and flattened. The meadow was awash in moonlight, and there, in the middle, five deer were feeding. Three were does. One was a young spike buck. The last was a king of his kind, large and strong, his antlers still in velvet but no less formidable. Ordinarily she would ignore him and concentrate on one of the does. But the new life demanded more meat, and the king buck had the most. His antlers were dangerous. They could kill. But her need eclipsed her caution. She would go for the monarch.

As yet, the deer were too far off. She instinctively gauged the distance. It would take five or six of her prodigious leaps to reach them, and by the second they would wheel and flee. It was unlikely she could catch them, not swollen and slow as she was.

She bared her fangs but didn't snarl. She must stay quiet and still and wait. She was good at waiting. She could lie in wait for prey for half a day or more if she had to.

The deer scent was intoxicating. She loved to slay deer more than she loved to slay anything. Badgers were plump and elk were succulent and squirrels were tasty treats, but nothing compared to the sweet juicy taste of raw deer meat. She craved it as no other.

The monarch and the others were drifting toward the aspens as they grazed. It would be a while before they were close enough. She held herself rigid with expectation, poised to released her power at the right instant. She was focused on the deer and only the deer, so when the bobcat scent reached her, she ignored it until she realized what it meant. She raised her head and turned it from side to side, testing the wind. The bobcat was to her left, but how close she couldn't be sure. She had seen him from a distance a few times, a big male who dared to hunt in her territory, but she had never been able to get close enough to kill him. Now here he was, stalking the same deer. He was probably after one of the does or the young spike. If he charged before she did, he would spoil everything. The king buck would be gone in the bat of an eyelid, and she would not have her meal.

She almost rose to stalk the bobcat, but the deer might hear or smell her. So she lowered her head and waited as they came slowly closer. Now she could reach them in three bounds, but she wanted them nearer still. She mustn't miss. Not with the new life she must nourish.

The moon rose higher and the wind grew stronger and she never twitched a muscle. She might have been made from stone. Her eyes were fixed intently on the king. She saw every flick of his ears, every quiver of his nostrils. He was wary, but then his kind always were. Wariness was as much a part of them as her need to slay them was part of her.

The spike and one of the does were now only two bounds way, but she didn't want them.

The bobcat scent was stronger. She flicked her eyes to the right and saw him; belly low to the ground, body primed to spring, concentrating on the deer as she was. The wind was from him to her, and he did not know she was there. She could be on him in a single leap, but the deer would bolt.

She watched the deer and the bobcat, both. She must be ready in case he charged.

The large buck was almost where she wanted him to be. A doe was so near she heard the crunch of teeth on grass. She could practically taste the warm, delicious blood that flowed in the buck's veins, and it took all her self-control to stay crouched.

The king raised his head toward the aspens.

She heard it, too. The *scritch* of the bobcat's claws as he dug into the ground for extra purchase. He was about to charge, about to spoil everything. She must attack first, and she must do it now or go hungry.

A golden streak in the night, she exploded into the meadow. Her first leap covered twenty feet, her second almost as much. She swept past the startled spike and a bleating doe and launched into the air as the king was turning to flee. She had judged perfectly and came down squarely on his back with her legs doubled under her and her paws splayed wide. Her claws sank deep into his flesh even as her fangs sought his neck. He snorted and took a bound, but her weight was too much and he stumbled. She tasted fur and then warm flesh and a spurt of hot blood filled her mouth. Her claws shredded fast and furious as she clung on and sought to bring him down. Only vaguely was she aware that the other deer were fleeing. Her prey bucked his whole body and almost threw her off, so strong was he. He took another bound, and this time he came down hard and his front legs buckled. He raked backward with his antlers, but she was just out of reach. She sank her fangs deeper and sliced with her claws in a razor frenzy.

The king snorted and heaved up, but he had lost too much blood and he only rose partway. His hind legs gave, and kicking and thrashing, he fell heavily onto his side.

She was awash in blood. There was a roaring in her ears and a tingle in her body. She bit down with all the strength in her jaws and the buck became still. She raised her head and glimpsed the white tails of the other deer as they melted into the forest on the far side of the meadow. She was about to lower her mouth to feed when she sensed she was not alone. She whirled, a snarl bursting from her in rage at the temerity of her challenger.

The bobcat was crouched at the edge of the aspens, a gray-brown form not a third her size but endowed with fangs and claws as lethal as her own. He had white at the throat and a bobbed tail. He growled and coiled, and the bob tail rose.

She flew at him in a fury. She was on him so fast that her first slash caught him on the shoulder. He didn't fight her. He ran. In a bolt of fur, he was in among the aspens. She started after him but stopped after only a few bounds. She would kill him another time. The new life must come first. The new life must come before everything.

She returned to the king of bucks. In death he wasn't so regal; his eyes were wide and glazing, and his tongue jutted from his mouth. She bit the tongue off and chewed hungrily. The tongue had a flavor all its own. As did the heart, her favorite part to eat. Lying on top of him, she fastened her fangs in his neck and lapped at the blood oozing from the wounds. She liked this, too: drinking until she was gorged with blood. Lapping and sucking and purring in contentment, she savored the reward of her prowess.

It was almost dawn when she left the kill. First

she kicked grass and dirt onto it to mark it as her own, and then she padded up through the aspens to the slope and leaped from boulder to boulder until she came to the ledge and her den, a declivity in the rock wide enough that she could stretch out at full length, and deep enough that it sheltered her from rain and snow and was invisible from below and above.

She lay on her side and closed her eyes. She wanted to sleep, but she was restless. It was the new life. Their time was near.

She got up and paced. Her restlessness grew. She moved to the lip of the ledge and gazed down over her domain. In the distance wolves howled, and she growled uneasily. To the east coyotes yipped. Somewhere in that vast sea of blackness a grizzly roared and everything else fell silent.

She kept on pacing. She could pace all night if she felt the compulsion, but all she felt now was a growing urge. The life inside her would not be denied, just as it would not be denied the previous times. Finally she lay facing the opening.

Her body told her when the moment had come. She yowled once and only once as the contractions rippled through her.

She licked the first of the kittens clean and then each one after that until five newborns groped feebly in the dark. She thought that was the end. She had never had more than five. Then a new pain racked her, a pain she never felt before when giving birth. She had to strain. She had to will her body to do what it always did naturally. The pain grew worse, and suddenly the deed was done and she lay back panting. A tiny mew brought her out of herself and she sat up.

The last one was different. She could tell that right away. It was more than twice as big as the others. It was also darker, much darker, the darkest kitten she ever had, so dark that even with her exceptional vision she had a hard time making it out. She licked it clean, the sour taste filling her mouth and the sour smell filling her nose. When she was done licking, she nudged the six of them close to her belly.

Their first nursing always hurt a little, but subsequent feedings were pleasant. Her life became a routine of eating to keep up her strength and feeding her brood. The king buck lasted four days. It would have lasted longer, but coyotes and ravens helped themselves when she was in the den with her young. From then on she made only short hunting forays. One night she treed a raccoon. It hissed and tried to bite her but was no match for her size and strength. Another night, she came on a shambling opossum. She did not like opossum meat much, but motherhood made her less particular.

Blind and helpless, her kittens clung to her when they fed and curled at her side when they slept. They were constantly mewing and touching her with their tiny paws. Their fur was covered with spots that would fade as they aged.

It was fourteen sleeps before the kittens opened their eyes. This young, their eyes were blue, but that, too, would change. When they were eight or nine moons old, their eyes would be a distinctive golden brown.

By now they could get around better, and now that they could see, the first thing they did was explore their surroundings, and the first thing they explored was her. They crawled up her and over her and around her until each knew her body as well as she did.

The next full moon she left the cave early, shortly after moonrise. By its light she could see almost as well as during the day. She was tired of small game and hungered for deer meat. Since giving birth, she had avoided the meadow but now she made straight for it.

The aspens quivered and glittered. She sniffed and listened, but the meadow was empty. Disappointed, she sank flat and waited with her extraordinary patience for the telltale sounds and odors that would herald the arrival of the deer. Instead, she smelled something else.

A black bear was crossing the meadow. Grunting and shuffling, it passed near where she lay and never saw or smelled her. She let it go unmolested. It was a big male and could inflict severe harm, and she had her kittens to think of.

Not long after the crackling of brush faded, a doe appeared. She smelled it before she saw it. Young and alone and incautious, the doe moved from the sanctuary of the trees to the open grass.

Rising in a crouch, the cat edged forward. She froze whenever the doe raised its head, which wasn't as often as a more mature doe would. The high grass hid her so well that she was within a single bound of her prey when the doe finally awakened to its peril. Uttering a bleat of terror, the doe wheeled to flee. She was on it in a bolt of golden lightning. Her claws raked deep. Her teeth found the jugular. She wanted to lie lapping the blood, but she gripped it by the neck and dragged it up through the aspens to the boulder-strewn slope below her haven. From the ledge she could see if any scavengers came close and drive them off.

She left the doe to check on her offspring. Five of the six were asleep. The sixth, the big one with the dark coat, was walking about exploring. She had never had a kitten do this so soon. He would be one to watch. She licked him and nosed him to the litter and then was out of the den and down the slope in stupendous leaps. Famished, she hunched over the doe and tore at the soft flesh and ate until she couldn't eat anymore. It was her first real meal since she gave birth, and new vitality coursed through her veins.

On returning to the den, she found the dark one up and about. She stretched out and offered her eight teats. The other kittens stirred and rose to feed. The dark one shouldered them aside and settled on her first. She didn't rebuke him. It was always this way. The weakest and the smallest were forced to fight for what they wanted or go hungry.

The warm feeling she always felt when she nursed came over her. She watched them suck, as content with life as she ever could be, and now and again she licked or nuzzled one or another.

All the next day she watched her kill as the kittens played on her and about her. Once a fox slunk out of the woods with its long nose raised to the breeze; it had caught the doe's scent. Her snarl sent it scampering. That evening when the kittens were sleeping, she descended and filled her belly.

The days and nights blended one into the other. Gradually the kittens gained strength and the courage to rove the den and the ledge. The dark one did it first, as he did everything first. His black coat, when he lay on her feeding, stood out against the gold of her own. She licked him more than the rest and at night let him curl under her chin.

Then came a day when strange sounds rose from the meadow. She sat up and beheld animals she had never seen before. They were as big as elk and seemed to have two heads. One of the heads was like that of elk but the other was unlike any head she had ever seen. To further confuse her, the second heads had long black hair and from some of the hair hung feathers. She had only ever seen feathers on birds, yet these strange creatures were plainly not birds.

Instinct caused her to flatten so that only her eyes and ears and nose were above the ledge. Instinct, too, caused a low snarl to issue from her throat—a snarl they were too far off to hear. But they were coming closer.

The strange beings came toward the aspens. Their hooves made heavy thuds in the earth. They stopped, and a bewildering thing happened—one of the creatures broke apart. The part that was on top, including a strange head with the black hair and a feather, separated from the part of the creature that looked like an elk.

The female realized that each of these strange beings was actually two creatures. The things with the black hair and feathers were on top of the elklike animals. Her tail twitched and she started to snarl again, but stopped. Something warned her not to let these creatures suspect she was there.

The one that had swung down was studying the ground. It came along with the others following and stopped at the bottom of the boulder-strewn slope. It had found the carcass of the doe and there was an excited exchange of noises between the creature on the ground and the creatures on the elklike animals.

They all looked up toward the ledge.

Chapter Two

The female sensed great danger. A growl started to rumble from her chest, but she stopped it and waited to see what the strange creatures would do. They were jabbering at each other like chipmunks, making noises new to her. The creature on the ground took a few steps up the slope but stopped at a sound from another of the creatures on one of the elklike animals. It seemed to her that the creature reluctantly turned back and climbed on the animal it had been riding, and together the whole strange group moved off into the woods toward the setting sun.

For the longest time she lay listening. She was fearful they would come back, and did not know why she was fearful. The only other time she had ever felt this way was when her mother was killed by the hunger-crazed wolves.

But the creatures did not return. Gradually the normal sounds of the forest returned, and she relaxed. Two of her kittens played with her tail, while two others wrestled and hissed. The big dark male paced back and forth and stared down at the alien world below. He was odd, the dark one. She had never had a kitten quite like him. For one thing, he always looked her in the eye when he came up to her. The others rarely did; they were too interested in her teats or her tail or her ears. For another thing, he was not only bigger but more muscular than the rest. By the time he was two months old, he had the build of a male of six months or more.

By then she weaned them from her milk. Their teeth were too sharp and it hurt when they sucked. Their claws, too, which they liked to flex when they nursed, pricked her belly uncomfortably. She started to bring her small kills to the den. The first was a rabbit. She plopped it down and five of the six were so startled they scrambled back in fear. Not the dark one. He walked up to the rabbit and sniffed and then sank his teeth into the rabbit's throat and sucked what little blood remained.

Another moon passed, and the kittens ate whatever she brought. They always fought over the meat and it was always the dark one who got the most. He brooked no disputes. One time when the second biggest male tried to wrest a piece of grouse away, the dark one cuffed him so hard he was nearly sent tumbling from the ledge.

At last came the day the female looked forward to, the day when she took them from the den for their first excursion in the outside world. Five of the six were scared and hugged her like a second pelt. The dark one walked at her side with the assurance of a yearling. He studied her every movement and imitated her with perfect ease. That night she licked him until he tired of being licked and moved off to curl up and sleep.

It was not long after that she came back one evening with a raccoon in her mouth. She leaped onto the ledge and found four of the six huddled in fright at the rear of the den. The dark one stood in front of the others, teeth bared, ready to defend the others. Belatedly, she realized that one of the females was missing. She sniffed and a snarl was torn from her throat.

The bobcat had been there.

She followed the scent up the mountain to a thicket. The missing female, or what was left, lay at the edge. From then on she was alert for the bobcat's presence, but he stayed away. He knew what she would do to him if she caught him.

Seven moons went by. Early one afternoon, she decided it was time for their first hunt. They were used to going short distances but not long treks, and several balked at entering the aspens. Not the dark one. He showed no fear of anything. She led them into the forest to a certain log. There she crouched. They followed her example, but they were still kittens and did not stay motionless, save for the dark one.

A short way off stood a tall tree. High in its branches was the conical nest of a gray squirrel that liked to come out at this time of day and forage. She had seen him many times. This day was no exception.

The dark one saw the squirrel right away. The rest were lax. One played with a pinecone. Two others pawed each other. A low hiss from her brought them close to the log where they peered over as she was doing.

The squirrel was perched on a limb, chattering noisily. Not at them but at the surrounding woods. It dropped onto all fours and scampered down the trunk, its bushy tail arched over its back.

Her kittens were riveted.

The squirrel was almost to the bottom. It moved in jerky spurts, stopping often.

Out of habit the female coiled and then let the tension drain from her. This was to be their kill if they were smart enough to sense what to do. Four of the litter, to her disappointment, didn't. They had never been this close to another living animal, and they were uncertain.

Not the dark one. He craned his neck over the log as the squirrel ran from cone to cone. Its antics brought it near the log. With a snarl, the dark one launched himself up and over. The squirrel raced for the tree. The dark one went after it, but that snarl had a high cost; the squirrel reached the tree first and was up the trunk in a flash, leaving the dark one thwarted and growling at the base. She was proud of him nonetheless. No kitten of hers ever went after prey its first time out.

It did not surprise her that he made the first kill not long after. A snake made the mistake of slithering onto the ledge during the hottest part of the day, no doubt to sun itself. It was only a bull snake, but it was thick and long and when the dark kitten leaped on it, the snaked bit and coiled and fought furiously for its life. The other kittens sprang to help, but it was the dark one that bit down on the head and ended the struggle.

The female had eaten snake a few times, but she was not fond of it. There was too little meat. She watched to see what the dark one would do—he sniffed the snake and walked off.

The rest of the kittens had a new toy. For days they played with the body, batting it around and pretending to stalk it and kill it. Finally the stink was more than she cared to endure and she carried it in her mouth down among the boulders and left it.

The days and nights rolled on, the moon waxed and waned. The kittens grew stronger and more sure of themselves as she showed them more of their world and taught them its dangers and delights. They tried to catch frogs at the lake. One of the kittens fell in and thrashed wildly until she plucked it out by the scruff of its neck. They swatted at fish in the stream. They chased birds and they chased chipmunks and they chased rabbits. One day they came on a turtle. It pulled into its shell and for the rest of the morning the kittens batted at the shell to make it roll end over end.

At night they lay on the ledge and listened to the baying of wolves and the fierce roar of the lords of the mountains. Occasionally they heard the far-off shriek of their own kind.

The leaves were starting to change color when she led them down through the aspens and across the meadow into the heavy timber. The thick canopy dappled the fallen leaves and pine needles with shadow, and maybe that was why she didn't see the snake when she passed a cluster of rocks. The kitten behind her saw it, and snarled and sprang. But it wasn't a bull snake. This one was a rattler. She heard the buzz of its tail and whirled, but by then the snake had sunk its fangs into the kitten's neck and went on striking. The dark one killed it. With a growl almost as loud as hers, the dark one did something she had never seen a kitten its size do; it crushed the rattlesnake's head with a swipe of a forepaw.

The kitten that had been bitten staggered and fell onto its side. She licked it and nosed it and then stood helpless as it convulsed and twitched and finally went limp.

The dark one did something else new. He walked up to his fallen brother and stared at the still form until she coughed to signal they should move on.

In due course the trees lost their leaves and the nights and days grew colder. Her small ones lost their kittenish traits and were more like her in appearance and acts. The dark one grew twice as fast as his siblings. He could run faster, leap farther. When they hunted, he stayed at her side and didn't trail behind as the others did.

The patterns of the other animals were changing. The deer and the elk drifted lower. The squirrels and chipmunks scurried about gathering stores. Bears sought to put as much fat on their bodies as they could.

On a cold, brisk morning she led the kittens farther down the mountain than they had ever gone, to a larger meadow where elk congregated in rutting season. The males bugled and fought over the females. They were not as alert as they normally were, and sometimes she could sneak close enough to bring one down. She always chose a female. The males were too big, their antlers formidable.

On this particular day she reached the meadow when the sun was directly overhead. She lay in a thicket with her young around her. No elk were there yet. It wasn't until the middle of the afternoon that a few cows drifted from cover. By late afternoon a herd of over fifty had gathered and the males commenced to fight. Their battles were spectacular; they would lower their heads and paw and charge, and the crash of their antlers was like the crash of a falling tree. Then they would dig in their hooves and push and strain until one or the other proved stronger. Sometimes their antlers locked and they become almost frantic in their efforts to break apart. The females huddled and watched, and it was then they were easiest to stalk.

The female crept to the meadow's edge, the dark one at her side. The other three—two males and a female—were behind her. She flattened and waited, and presently a cow drifted near. Coiling her legs, she launched in long leaps and vaulted high onto the cow's back. Her weight was enough to bring down a deer, but elk were a lot bigger and although this one staggered, it stayed upright and bawled in fright and tried to shake her off. She churned her claws, threshing hide and flesh, even as she sank her fangs deep. She was aware of the dark one clinging to the cow's neck and the other kittens attacking its legs. With a loud cry, the cow toppled. The other female elk and most of the bulls scattered.

Most, but not all.

She didn't see the one until it was almost on top of them. With her lightning reflexes, she sprang clear. The bull hooked his antlers at the dark one, and the dark one jumped higher than she ever saw a male its age jump, and avoided being impaled. The bull slashed at another male, but it wasn't as quick. It shrieked as the sharp tines drove into its body. The bull tossed it a good distance and the instant it fell hard to the earth it was up and running. She did the same, the rest on her flanks. The bull came after them but stopped at the end of the meadow and snorted and stamped.

She did not like being driven from her prey. She could see the cow, still down and bleeding badly, its legs moving feebly. Then she heard a mew and turned to find the male kitten the bull had attacked was down, too, and bleeding as badly as the cow, if not worse. She went to him. There were holes in his body and another in his neck. He raised his head and mewed at her and she licked him, but that was all she could do. His eyes closed and he convulsed a few times and then he lay limp.

She had lost another. It was always thus. Out of every litter, it was rare if two survived.

The bull continued to stamp and snort and was joined by others. Their rut was temporarily forgotten in their united effort against a common enemy.

She started back up the mountain. Their bellies were empty, and she was in an angry mood. She was almost glad when they startled a doe into flight. The dark one was on it before she was, but together they brought the doe down and it was the dark one whose fangs dealt the kill. Afterward, they feasted and then retired to a sunny clearing to rest.

The other male and the young female still had kittenish streaks, and played and wrestled. Not the dark one. He lay watching everything around them, and missed nothing. She went over and licked him, and he licked her and she lay at his side.

The hunting was good until the first heavy snow. She had seen snow many times and was accustomed to it, but to her young it was wondrous. They frolicked and gamboled, even the dark one, swatting and rolling and acting as if they were one moon old again.

Game became scarce. Many of the smaller animals stayed in their burrows and dens. Bears were in hibernation. Most of the birds so common in the summer were gone. Ravens and jays stayed, but they were too wary to be caught. Grouse went deeper into the thickets and were harder to find. Rabbits changed color and were harder to spot. The deer were not abroad as much.

Where before she and her brood might have gone three or four days between kills, now it was sometimes five or six. They were often hungry. The temperature fell, so they were often cold, too. They spent much of their time at the den, resting and gazing down over their domain.

This winter was worse than most, and in the coldest of the moons she was pressed to find prey. She roved far and wide without success.

They had been four and a half days without anything to eat when she caught the scent of a doe, mixed with blood. Her belly brushing the snow, she stalked through the undergrowth until she saw it. Puzzled, she stopped.

The doe hung by its neck from a tree. A thin snakelike thing that was not alive had been wrapped around the doe's neck and head and around a low limb.

The female had never seen anything like this, and she was wary.

Beside her, the dark one crouched silent and still. The other two were famished and eager to eat. They kept shifting their weight and flicking their tails, and finally the male snarled and moved toward the doe.

She tried to move in front of him, but he went around her and kept going, his paws sinking into the soft snow. She was uneasy. Something was wrong. She sensed danger.

The dark one growled. He was looking at a snowbank near the doe. She looked but could not account for his growl.

The other male came to the doe. He walked in a small circle around her, looking up and growling. She was well out of reach. Crouching, he prepared to leap.

The female went to rise. She had been wrong about the danger. They could all feed.

That was when the snowbank broke apart and a two-legged creature with a feather in its black hair reared up.

Chapter Three

There was a *twang*. The young male leaped high into the air and screamed in pain. A feathered shaft jutted from his body. Even as he alighted, another shaft struck him.

Other two-legged creatures rushed from behind snow-covered trees and burst from hiding places.

The female whirled and ran. The dark one was her shadow. Behind them loped the smaller female. A feathered shaft sought them but missed. She did not stop to look back until she was on a rise well out of reach of the feathered shafts. The two-legged creatures had surrounded the fallen male and were poking him with a stick.

Now only the two were left.

The dark one and the young female grew in size and strength. The young female was not yet as big as the mother, but the dark one had surpassed her size and was still growing.

On a sunny day when the snow had melted away and the promise of warm weather was in the air, she was leading them along a ridge when the dark one suddenly broke away and loped down the other side. His nose was close to the ground and when she lowered hers she caught the same scent. She ran faster to catch up, but he was going full out and he increased his lead. She burst out of the trees, and ahead he was a black blur streaking toward the source of the scent.

The bobcat heard the pad of paws and tried to run, but the dark one was on him before he took more than several bounds. The bobcat whirled, and the dark one slammed into him, shoulder against shoulder. Both went down in a tumbling, snarling, clawing melee. The dark one was bigger, but the bobcat was older and the veteran of many combats. Their fight was fierce. The female crouched ready to leap in, but she never had an opening. They rolled and raked with their claws and bit and snapped until a piercing cry rent the air.

All movement ceased.

The dark one was holding the bobcat by the neck, and the bobcat was limp. He let the bobcat drop and walked off without looking back. His body was a welter of cuts. The tip of his left ear had been bitten off and his throat was bleeding, but the wound wasn't deep. He spent the next seven sleeps recuperating and was soon restored to vigor.

Spring arrived, and the forest pulsed with game galore. The female and the other two hunted and ate well.

In the evenings she would lie on the ledge with the dark one and the young female and listen to the sounds from below. One evening the sounds were unlike any she had ever heard. Curious, she rose and worked her way down the slope. Neither the dark one nor the female came with her. She skirted the meadow and went down the mountain to the edge of the flatland and beheld a sight that caused her skin to prickle. Scores of two-legged creatures were erecting high cones of buffalo hides and saplings. They had many of the animals that looked like elk but were not elk.

Unease filled her, and she rumbled deep in her chest. She did not like this. They were a distance from her den, but there were many of them, and she had not forgotten what they did to her young male that day in the snow.

Turning, she slunk away. She wanted nothing to do with them.

They became nuisances. During the day they were everywhere, riding their elklike animals or walking about. They never went anywhere alone but always in pairs, or more. They jabbered a lot and had an odd scent.

Once she was stalking a doe and a group of them rode near and scared the doe off. She was hidden in the brush, and they came close to her without realizing she was there. She could have leaped out and slain a few, but she remembered the feathered shafts and stayed hidden.

Another time she was following a stream and she came on a number of two-legged females who were dipping hides in the water and wringing them out. They chirped without cease and annoyed her considerably, but she left them be.

On a day not long after, a commotion drew her to the flatland. The creatures were taking down the conical hides and folding them and placing them on poles attached to the elklike animals. She didn't realize they were leaving until they formed into a long line and made off to the east. It pleased her to see them go. The forest was hers again, hers and her remaining offspring's.

The dark one had taken to hunting by himself. Sometimes he was gone for several sleeps. She would miss him, and pace.

The young female was always there. Sometimes they hunted together and at other times she went one way and the young female another.

Summer crawled into autumn and the aspens became splashes of bright colors. The beaver were busy with their dams and the bull elk were bugling again and bears were stuffing themselves.

On a morning when frost covered the ground and her breath formed tiny clouds, she and the female went hunting. They drifted apart, as had become their wont. She was threading through a stand of alders when her ears caught the crunch of teeth. Flattening, she stalked toward the sound and discovered a solitary doe, grazing. The doe was facing the alders, so she circled to come at it from the side. As it happened she turned into the wind and caught the scent of other predators that had the same idea she did: wolves.

She could not tell how many, but there was more than one. They were on the other side of the doe, converging. She remembered her mother, and before she could stop it a growl escaped.

The doe raised its head and pricked its long ears and looked anxiously around.

Simultaneously from out of the high grass sprang four wolves. They were on the doe at her first spring and brought her down in concert; one leaped at her throat and the others at her legs. The doe stood no chance.

The female was ablaze with rage. They had stolen her prey. They were four and she was one and that should have deterred her but it didn't. She was on them in a whirlwind of teeth and claws. She drove them from the doe, but once they were over their initial surprise, they laid back their ears and snarled and growled, prepared to fight for their meal.

The bloodlust was on her. The largest male wolf leaped and she met him in midair and opened his shoulder. He opened her leg. No sooner did she set herself than two others came at her from both sides. She drove one off with a flashing paw, but the other ripped her flank open and sprang out of reach.

They circled her.

She had made a grave mistake. She was more than a match for any single wolf, or even two, but certainly not four. Their numbers would be her downfall. Unless she fled, they would overwhelm her and bring her down.

She stayed. A compulsion had come over her, a willingness to fight to the death even if the death was hers. She crouched and her snarls rivaled theirs in a savage din.

The large male came at her and she swung her front paw. He dodged. Pain seared her hindquarters. In a flash she whirled and caught the culprit across the chest. More pain in her side, and she spun and tore a female wolf. They didn't relent. Again and again they came at her, and again and again she drove them off. But each time cost her and although she inflicted wound after wound, they were four and she was one. They were wearing her down. She felt it, and they sensed it, and they closed in for the kill.

The cat had been bitten and clawed severely. She was bleeding and torn. A leap would carry her over them, but she crouched and snarled and then they were on her, four at once, and they bore her down and tore at her undersides. Slavering jaws gaped to clamp on her throat.

Suddenly a dark fury was among them. Strong blows sent each of the wolves tumbling. The large male wolf tried to rise, but the dark one was on him in a bound and bit into the back of his neck. The *crunch* of bone was sharp and loud. Before the body fell, the dark one was on the others, slashing and snapping. Such was the force of his attack that all three turned and ran rather than fight. He stood glaring and growling after them. When the sounds of their flight faded, he turned and stepped to the doe and began to eat.

She let him. It was her kill, but she moved to one side and licked her many wounds until he was done. Then she ate her own fill. When they made for the den, she followed him.

She spent a restless night. Many of the bites and cuts were deep, and whether she lay on her belly or either side, the pain kept her awake. Toward dawn she dozed and was awakened a few hours later by the squawk of a jay. The dark one was on the ledge. She went and stretched out next to him and only then did she realize that the young female had not returned. It was to be expected. She gave birth to them and nurtured them and taught them, and eventually there came a day when they struck off on their own. Occasionally one wouldn't want to leave and she had to persuade it.

The dark one showed no inclination to go just yet. That pleased her.

The next day she went to a stream for water, but that was her only excursion. That night she slept a little better.

Within five moons she was well enough to hunt. She was in no shape to try to bring down a deer, so she settled for an incautious squirrel. It did little more than whet her appetite. When she got back she found a deer haunch on the ledge and the dark one asleep. She ate until she was gorged and slept until the next day. When she woke she felt almost like her old self.

Another winter froze the land. The snow was deeper than most winters, and she and the dark one spent much of their time in the den.

One evening she killed a doe and cached it. She returned the next day to feed on the carcass only to find a wolverine had laid claim to her kill. It looked up and bared its fangs. It wasn't as big as she was and barely half her weight, but she had encountered its kind before. Of all the animals in the wilderness, wolverines were the fiercest. Even grizzlies gave way for them. She bared her own fangs and then discreetly retreated.

The winter was long and hard. The cold froze the lakes and the streams were sloughs of ice. She and the dark one had to range wide and far to find enough meat to sustain them, and at that it was barely enough.

A new spring restored their world. On a bright afternoon, she and the dark one were prowling a high ridge near the old den of a brown bear. A marmot spotted them and whistled. She didn't stalk it. When she was young she had tried to catch them, but marmots always disappeared down into their holes before she could get close.

She and the dark one moved along a trail once used by the great bear. She came to a short piece of wood jutting from the ground and sniffed at it, puzzled by the faintest of vague odors. The dark one came and sniffed, too. He took a step past her and she heard a *snap* and suddenly he sprang into the air, screeching with pain. His left forepaw was caught in something that had been covered with leaves and dirt, and the paw was spurting blood. He snarled at it and twisted and pulled and wrenched, but his paw wouldn't come free.

She was bewildered. This was new to her, and frightening. The thing that held him was hard like rock, but it was not like any rock she knew. To add to her bewilderment, it had sharp fangs that held the dark one fast. Small circles of the same hard material connected it to the short piece of wood. She tried to bite through but couldn't.

The dark one renewed his efforts. He became near frantic. He snarled and screeched and leaped and pulled. She began to despair of ever freeing him when he threw himself up the bank and twisted his whole body, and suddenly his paw was free. Or half of it was. The rest stayed clamped in the hard teeth. He limped away and when she headed for the den he limped after her.

By the next morning the dark one's leg was swollen and he could barely stand. A thick yellow pus oozed from the wound. He licked and licked, but it did his paw little good.

She thought she would lose him. For five sleeps he stayed on the ledge on his side. When she nosed him he didn't move. His paw was a ruin. It was only half the size as before; only two claws were left. On the sixth day he sat up. She caught a grouse and shared it, but he ate little. She ambushed a fox and brought it back. The meat was stringy, but it was better than an empty stomach.

The dark one crawled to the stream. He drank and lowered his paw in and lay there the rest of the day. She stayed near, watching over him. When a pair of coyotes happened along, she chased them off.

That night the dark one limped back to the den. He slept until the sun was high in the sky the next day and limped down to the stream to drink and soak his paw. He did the same the day after. The pus stopped oozing and the swelling went down and he could move a little faster.

She killed a small doe and brought it to him. The dark one ate and then she ate and between them there wasn't much left. The dark one slept some more. About the middle of the night she got up and went to the meadow and lay in wait until sunrise for deer to show, but none did. When she climbed back to the den, the dark one was gone.

The morning sun was warm, and she dozed. When it was straight overhead she rose and yawned and arched her back. The dark one still wasn't back. She went to the stream, but he wasn't there. She went to the meadow, but he wasn't there. She roved wide, but found no trace of him.

That night she heard a grizzly roar and wolves howl and a lynx shriek, but she did not hear any of her own kind. She did not hear the dark one.

At daybreak she was on the move. No deer were at the meadow, so she ventured down the mountain to another. Half a dozen does were feeding. She got upwind and crept to within leaping range.

Suddenly the deer raised their heads and looked right at her. Or so she thought until a noise came from behind her. She was rising when there was a sharp pain in her side and she was jolted half around.

For a few heartbeats she was rooted by the sight of a feathered shaft sticking out of her. Wheeling, she went to race off, but another pain shot through her and she pitched forward. The meadow and the sky changed places. She struggled to rise, but her front legs wouldn't work.

Dimly, the female was aware of two-legged creatures with long black hair closing on her, and of their excited jabber. She raised her head and snarled at one and he held a bent limb and a feathered shaft toward her. A barbed tip was close to her eye. She tried to bite him.

A vast blackness consumed her.

Part Two

The Call of the Family

Chapter Four

The whites called them Sheepeater Indians because they ate a lot of mountain sheep. They also ate a lot of elk and deer and whatever else they could kill and forage, but the white name stuck.

They called themselves the Tukaduka. In the white tongue it meant "people of the high places." They preferred the high parks and valleys to the flatlands and low valleys and seldom drifted down from the heights.

Other tribes considered them poor. They did not have horses. They did not have buffalo-hide lodges. They did not have white guns or white blankets or white pots and pans. They did not have white knives or white sewing needles or any of the other thousand and one things the whites had that the other tribes craved. But that was fine by the Tukaduka. They did not envy the whites their many goods. They did not desire to be rich as the other tribes saw rich to be.

To the Tukaduka, richness lay in the simple life. Getting along with others was valued more than all else, even white guns. Devotion to family meant more than white knives or sewing needles. Their families, the whites would say, were everything to them.

They did not live in villages. Each family had its own valley or park and dwelled in perfect contentment. It was true that at times they went hungry. It was true that the icy cold of winter was hard and sometimes cost lives. But they were happy, and to the Tukaduka being happy was the reason Coyote had brought them into the world.

War parties from other tribes left them alone. Counting coup on the Tukaduka, the other tribes believed, was as easy as plucking grass. It was insulting for a Piegan or a Blackfoot to boast of killing one. The Tukaduka were regarded as meek and weak as the sheep the whites named them after.

So the Sheepeaters lived quiet, simple lives, and went about their daily tasks at peace with the other tribes and the world around them.

Two Knives was a father of three. His family dwelled in a small valley watered by a gurgling stream high near the Divide. He had seen white men only twice. The first time it had been a party of trappers who stopped in the valley for the night. They were after beaver. Two Knives told them there were none in his valley, but they didn't believe him until they had scoured the banks of the stream from one end of the valley to the other. One night two of them got drunk and tried to force themselves on Dove Sings. That angered Two Knives greatly. He was not big enough or strong enough to fight them, but fortunately another white man thought it wrong and stopped them.

The second time had been better. A lone white man with hair like snow stopped for a night. He shared his supper and was kind and smiling. Two Knives liked him a lot and could not understand why other Indians had given the white man the name Wolverine. The man had been as peaceful as the birds that Dove Sings was named after.

Much of what the white man said, Two Knives did not understand. The man had something called a "book," which he recited with a flourish of his hands and arms. It amused Dove Sings greatly. Two Knives had been considerably surprised when Wolverine told him that the whites kept much of their learning and their wisdom in those "books." Two Knives always thought that learning and wisdom were best kept inside a person.

Even to this day Two Knives occasionally remembered Wolverine and wondered what became of him. Wolverine had been good and decent, qualities Two Knives admired more than any others.

That had been many winters ago, when the oldest of their children was a baby. By now Fox Tail had lived nearly twenty winters and would soon take a wife of his own and move away. Two Knives was not looking forward to that. He would miss his oldest son dearly. He loved his other two children just as much, but it was always hard on the heart when a dear one left.

Otherwise, all was well with their world. Their lodge, made of pine boughs and brush, was spacious enough that they weren't cramped. Each evening the five of them sat around the small fire and talked. On this particular evening their eyelids were heavy with the need for sleep. Soon they would turn in.

Elk Running, the middle child, was telling them about how he had nearly caught a fish in a pool with his hands. The fish had proved too quick, and he had slipped and fallen in, and they were smiling and laughing when they all heard the shriek. It pierced the valley like a knife thrust, silencing the coyotes and the owls, and silencing all of them, as well. They sat frozen in surprise as the shriek wavered on the wind and gradually faded.

"One of the big cats," Dove Sings said.

"It is looking for a mate," Two Knives guessed. "By morning it will be gone."

"I hope so," little Bright Rainbow said. "That scared me."

Dove Sings took their youngest onto her lap and smoothed her hair, comforting her. "The big cats do not bother us if we do not bother them. We will be fine."

Two Knives said, "It is the brown bears you must watch out for. When you see one, climb a tree as high as you can climb."

"I am not afraid of them," Elk Running declared.

"You should be." Two Knives had lost a cousin to a brown bear. His cousin lingered for days with half his face bitten off and half his chest torn to ribbons. Two Knives's secret fear was that one day a brown bear would catch him as it had his luckless cousin.

"I will look for sign tomorrow," Fox Tail announced.

"The cat will be gone," Two Knives stressed.

"I will look anyway. It is not often we find cat sign."

Two Knives was proud of his oldest's tracking skill. His son would sometimes spend half a day tracking an animal for the fun of tracking. "Be careful."

"I am always careful," Fox Tail said.

The next morning started like any other. They were up at the first blush of dawn. Dove Sings made a breakfast of grouse eggs and strips of sheep meat.

Fox Tail took his bow and quiver and went off to search for sign of the big cat.

Two Knives spent the morning helping Dove Sings cure a deer hide. Unlike some of the other tribes, the Tukaduka did not think it beneath a man's dignity to do what other tribes called "women's work." He and Dove Sings did nearly everything together. Sometimes he even cooked their meals.

The sun was at its highest when Dove Sings looked up and remarked, "He should have been back by now."

Two Knives did not need to ask who she was talking about. Elk Running was over by the stream with Bright Rainbow. "The cat was high up. Fox Tail could spend most of the day looking and not find anything." The big cats did not leave a lot of sign as other animals did; they were too stealthy, too secretive.

"I wish he had not gone."

"You are worried?"

"Yes. Here." Dove Sings touched her bosom over her heart.

"I will go look for him."

"No," Dove Sings said. "You are probably right. The cat is gone and he is safe and I worry over nothing. I would rather you stay here with us."

"As you want." But now Two Knives was worried. His wife often had feelings she could not account for that turned out to be right. He spent the rest of the afternoon constantly glancing at the forested slopes that rimmed their valley and were in turn capped by ramparts of stone or in the case of the highest peaks, by cones and spires of glistening snow.

The sun was low on the horizon when Elk Running came to him and asked, "Shouldn't Fox Tail have been back by now?"

"It could be your brother found sign and followed it," Two Knives suggested. He did not mention that Fox Tail knew better than to be abroad after dark. The Tukaduka were *never* abroad after dark.

"Fox Tail is strong and brave. Maybe he will slay the cat and bring us the hide."

"Maybe," Two Knives said.

Dusk settled over their valley. They ate supper and sat around the fire, all of them quiet, and listened. Coyotes yipped and a wolf howled and near their lodge an owl hooted.

"Fox Tail would never be gone this long." Dove Sings voiced what was on all their minds.

"I will look for him in the morning," Two Knives said.

He did not sleep well. Nor did his wife. Usually they slept cuddled together, but on this night they turned and tossed and for long stretches he lay on his back and stared at the empty air, worried. He was up much earlier than was his wont, and dressed and went out. The brisk chill made him shiver. He gazed at the stars and out over the valley, and frowned.

A doeskin dress whispered, and Dove Sings was beside him. "Something has happened to him."

"I think so, yes," Two Knives admitted.

"You should not go alone. Take Elk Running."

"Bright Rainbow and you should not be alone."

"I can use a bow, and I have my knife."

"I want him to stay with you," Two Knives insisted. He seldom forced his will on her, but in this he was firm.

Dove Sings took his hand in hers. "We have lived many winters together. I would not like to live a winter alone."

Two Knives smiled. "I am not a Shoshone. I do not test my manhood with my courage."

"I will not sleep until you return."

His stomach was in no shape for breakfast. He left shortly after sunup armed with his small bow and short arrows and a pair of flint knives. Dove Sings filled a pouch with dried deer meat, and he slanted the strap across his chest. She and Elk Running and Bright Rainbow stood and watched him jog off. He looked back at them right before he entered the trees, and Dove Sings waved. He waved to them.

The forest was eerily quiet. Normally birds warbled and squirrels chattered, but today not a single chirp or chitter broke the stillness. Even the wind had died and the trees were motionless and foreboding.

Two Knives did not like to think what it might mean. The shriek the night before had come from the north, and it was to the north end of the valley that he bent his steps. His moccasins made little noise on the carpet of pine needles, but each sound they did make was like a thunderclap to his ears. He walked with an arrow notched to the sinew string.

The higher Two Knives climbed, the steeper the slopes. He suspected that the cat had entered their valley through a pass in the north ring of peaks. If so, that was the smart place to start looking for sign. It was where his son would have looked.

By midmorning Two Knives could see the pass, still a ways off. The next slope was mostly barren of vegetation. Years ago an avalanche had torn most of the growth away, and it was just starting to reclaim the soil. He started up and there, in the dirt, was a footprint he knew as well as he did the wrinkles in his palm. "Fox Tail," he said out loud. The footprints pointed up. He eagerly followed them and was almost to a broad belt of firs when the footprints changed direction. The reason was another set of tracks that came down from above and turned toward the valley floor. His son had followed them

Two Knives stopped in consternation. The tracks were plainly those of one of the big cats—but he had never in his life seen or heard of cat tracks as big as these. The tracks were almost as big as young brown bear tracks. Sinking onto a knee, he tried to cover one with his outspread hand and couldn't. He was more than a little afraid. "Fox Tail, no," he said. His son should know better than to follow a cat that big.

He hurried on into thick woods where it was harder to find sign. He had to go slow and stay bent low to the ground. Only once did he come across a complete set of the cat's prints, all four paws in a row; they confirmed something he had noticed. The cat was limping. He attributed the cause to the fact that one of the front paws was smaller than the other three.

Shadows dappled the greenery. Silence reigned saved for the buzz of a fly that flew around Two Knives's head and then winged off. He stepped over a log and skirted several spruce. Ahead was a boulder larger than his lodge. He went around it, as the tracks did, and on the far side drew up short. His chest seemed to burst outward and his breath caught in his lungs. "No!" he said.

Fox Tail lay on his back. Most of his throat was gone. A gaping cavity and puncture marks showed where the cat had ripped it out with its teeth. Fox Tail's stomach had also been torn open and his intestines strewn about as if the cat were in a frenzy of vicious glee. Fox Tail's glazed eyes were locked wide in surprise.

The tracks told Two Knives the story. His son had come around the boulder and the cat had been waiting, crouched on a niche well above Two Knives's head, a niche that only the sinuous cat could reach. Two Knives figured that Fox Tail had been so intent on the tracks that he had not noticed the cat until it was too late. Fox Tail's broken bow was next to him. His quiver had been torn apart and the arrows scattered and bit in half.

Two Knives bowed his head. His eyes misted and he had a lump in his throat. He put a hand on his dead son and said tenderly, "I loved you with all that I am." He did not want to leave the body there, but he could not take it back either; he would spare Dove Sings the horrible sight. Accordingly, he gathered fallen limbs and dry brush and rocks and covered his son so that scavengers could not get at the remains.

Two Knives had a decision to make: go after the cat or go back. He turned and headed down. Too many obstacles and too many thickets delayed him. It seemed to take forever to descend to the valley floor. He came out of the pines and broke into a run. The high grass swished about his legs and he startled a rabbit that bounded off in fright. He was still a long distance from the lodge when he noticed the grass to his right about twenty steps away swaying as if with the wind—only there was no wind. He stopped, and the grass stopped moving.

For the second time that day Two Knives shivered, but not from cold. He raised his bow and strained his ears but heard only the hammering of his heart. Time crawled. Finally he made bold to move on, and with his first step the grass bent. He stopped moving again and so did the grass. A tingle ran down his spine.

There could be no doubt.

The cat was stalking him.

Chapter Five

Two Knives stood rooted in dismay. He had never had anything like this happen. He raised his bow and sighted down the arrow at the moving grass. He didn't see the cat. It must be crouched low. He waited for it to show itself, but it didn't.

Should he stay there and wait the beast out or try and make it to his lodge? He liked the second idea best, but the cat might follow him, imperiling those he loved most in the world.

A low snarl warned him the cat hadn't gone anywhere. He backed toward the forest, and the grass moved as if to invisible hands, bending in the direction he was going. In frustration he almost let loose his shaft.

Two Knives slid one foot behind him and then the other. The grass caught at his ankles, and he was careful not to stumble. The bow string dug into his fingers, but he didn't relax it.

In his wake stalked the cat.

Two Knives did not sweat often, but he sweated now. Drops beaded his brow, and his buckskin shirt became so wet it clung to him. He risked a glance behind him and saw he had a long way to go to the trees. With the cat shadowing his every step, it would be a wonder if he made it.

Two Knives thought of Fox Tail. A great sadness gripped him. He had loved his firstborn with all the love a father could have for a son. He loved his other children, too. In order to spare them and Dove Sings, he decided to provoke the cat into attacking him and then to try and slay it with an arrow. He came to the forest. Farther in, the undergrowth was thick, but here at the edge there was little. He would see the cat if it came at him. He backed up a dozen shrot steps and raised his bow. He saw the tips of the grass move, but they stopped moving well out from the woods. He aimed at the spot where he thought the cat must be and let fly. The shaft flew true and hit exactly where he wanted, but nothing happened. There was no screech or yowl, no rush of a tawny form with fangs bared. He had missed and wasted an arrow.

Two Knives nocked another. Acting on an idea, he sidestepped to a tall pine. Without taking his eyes off the grass, he jumped high into the air and wrapped his arm around one of the lowest branches. In another moment he was straddling it and had the bow string drawn. He could see more of the grass—but he still couldn't see the cat.

Two Knives climbed higher. He went as high as the limbs would bear his weight and still couldn't spot his stalker. He could see his lodge, though. Dove Sings and Bright Rainbow were moving about outside it. He went to cup a hand to his mouth to shout a warning to them to go inside but thought better of it. Dove Sings might do the opposite and come to see what was wrong. She was strong willed, that woman.

Two Knives turned his attention to the grass again, and his blood turned to ice in his veins. The grass had parted, framing the head and forequarters of the meat-eater. He could not quite believe what he was seeing. It wasn't a tawny mountain cat; it was a *black* one, as black as a raven, with piercing yellow eyes that were fixed on him in hatred. He saw it for only a moment, and then it was gone.

Two Knives had never heard of such a thing. Or had he? He remembered a tale told among his people, a tale he'd heard when he was a small boy, about a black mountain cat like this one that wreaked havoc with the Tukaduka. The Devil Cat, they called it. Not in the white sense, which Two Knives had learned from one of the trappers. The trapper said that all the good in the world came from God and all the bad in the world came from what the trapper called the Devil. Apparently the white Devil lived far under the earth in an inferno of fire and caused suffering to human souls after death.

The Tukaduka meaning was different. To them a devil was a thing of evil, whether it be man or animal. The Devil Cat of their legend was a beast of unrivaled bloodlust that thirsted to kill, kill, kill. When it died, its spirit lived on to continue killing, and to this day Tukaduka mothers sometimes warned their children not to be out after dark or the Devil Cat would get them.

Two Knives had not taken the legend seriously, until now. He hoped for another glimpse, but the creature had disappeared. It had been looking right at him, so he saw no point in trying to hide. Instead, he descended to the lowest limb, hung by an arm, and dropped.

The cat didn't show itself.

Two Knives put his back to the trunk. He would have a clear target in front, and the cat could not get at him from the rear. But as more time passed and the shadows lengthened and nothing happened, it occurred to him that the Devil Cat might be waiting for dark to fall. At night it would be hard to see it, if not impossible. He would be at the beast's mercy.

Two Knives glanced down the valley. Should he fall prey to the cat's claws, his family would be next. If he was to make a stand, why not make it where it mattered most? His feet acquired wings. He flew along the tree line, and off in the grass there was movement. He didn't understand why the Devil Cat didn't attack, but he was glad it didn't. He ran and ran. His legs hurt and his chest ached, but he didn't stop. He ran farther than he had since he was a young man of twenty winters.

Dove Sings and Bright Rainbow were not in sight, but Elk Running was behind the lodge pleating a grass rope.

"Go inside!" Two Knives shouted. "Go inside quick!"

Elk Running did not ask why. Two Knives had taught his children from an early age the importance of doing as he told them in times of danger, and Elk Running obeyed.

The waving grass kept pace with Two Knives. He flew around to the front of the lodge and reached the elk-hide flap just as Dove Sings was coming out with her own bow in her hands.

"What is wrong? Why did you send Elk Running inside?

Two Knives did something he had never done before; he pushed her and barreled inside after her. Quickly, he lowered and tied the flap, knowing full well it wouldn't stop a mountain cat the size of the black one.

"What is it?" Dove Sings asked in rising alarm.

"Devil Cat," Two Knives said.

She looked at him as if she thought he couldn't possibly be serious. "What are you talking about?"

Two Knives didn't take his eyes off the flap. He stepped back and drew the bow string to his cheek. "A black cat as big as two tawny ones. It killed Fox Tail, and now it is after me."

"Fox Tail is dead?" Dove Sings swayed and her hand rose to her throat.

Elk Running and Bright Rainbow shared her shock. The boy recovered first and came to his father's side with his bow ready. "We will kill it together, Father."

Two Knives was going to say no and tell the boy to move back, but two arrows were better than one. "Everyone be still."

Outside their lodge, complete silence fell. It was so quiet that Two Knives could hear the hammering of his heart. He was afraid for his family. He was very afraid.

Then, with awful slowness, the elk hide bulged inward. Only a little way, then stopped. Two Knives could not tell whether it was the Devil Cat's head or a paw. He was rigid with dread and his lungs would not work. He imagined the cat ripping through the hide and springing on them and tearing right and left with its claws and teeth.

Bright Rainbow gasped.

The hide was bulging again. The Devil Cat pressed harder, but the tie held and the hide only gave a hand's width. The cat expressed its annoyance at being thwarted with a snarl. The bulge went away.

Two Knives aimed at where the cat had been

pressing. His arrow would penetrate the hide. With luck it would also penetrate the cat's skull. He drew the string as far back as he could without it breaking. Barely breathing, he held the arrow steady. His arm began to feel the strain. The hide didn't bulge. He was focused on the spot where it had been and only on that spot. Dove Sings said something, but he did not hear what it was. The hide still didn't bulge. His shoulder hurt, but he refused to slacken the string. He willed his arm to hold it steady. Had the Devil Cat left? he wondered. The string was digging into his fingers, but he didn't loosen his pressure on the arrow. Then suddenly the hide bulged and he went to release, but Elk Running's bow twanged before his and the arrow struck the hide slightly to the left of the bulge, missing the head and causing the Devil Cat to draw back and vent a shriek of fury.

"I think I hit it!" Elk Running exclaimed.

Two Knives very much doubted it, but he kept his doubt to himself. "You did fine, son." He let up on his own bow for a few moments to relieve his arm, then drew the arrow back again. Another long wait ensued. The hide stayed smooth. After a while Dove Sings came up and put a hand on his shoulder.

"It has gone."

Two Knives doubted that, too. To find out, he lowered his bow and edged to the flap and undid the tie enough to peer out. The trampled area in front of the lodge was clear. The cat could be crouched on either side or in the high grass.

"Do we go after it, Father?" Elk Running asked.

"We do not."

"But it killed Fox Tail."

"One death is enough." Two Knives secured the

tie and went to the fire and sat facing the hide and put the bow at his side, the arrow still notched.

Without being asked, Dove Sings brought the water skin over and offered it to him. "What is your plan?"

"We will stay in all night. If it has not come back by morning, then maybe it is safe."

"And if it does?"

"We will do what we can."

"You have the lance," Dove Sings reminded him.

Two Knives had forgotten about it. The summer previous they had gone over into the next valley after elk and come on an old camp made by a hunting party. He'd found a lance near the embers of a fire and by its marking recognized it as Shoshone. The tip and about half an arm's length had broken off and whoever owned it had left it. He'd brought it back and sharpened the end. It wasn't as long as before, but it was sturdy and thick and made for a good weapon in close quarters.

Dove Sings brought it over and laid it on his other side.

"Thank you."

Elk Running was pacing. "Maybe it will bleed to death," he said.

"You should sit and rest," Two Knives advised. "It will be a long night."

"I am not tired." Elk Running gestured angrily. "I wish Fox Tail were here. I will miss him."

Two Knives closed his eyes and bowed his head, remembering.

Dove Sings touched his cheek. "How bad was it?"

"Bad."

"Do you think he hurt the Devil Cat before it killed him?"

Two Knives hadn't considered that at all. "Possibly," he said. There had been a lot of dried blood, which he had assumed was his son's.

"Would you like to eat?"

Two Knives was famished, but the idea held no appeal. "Maybe later," he answered.

Bright Rainbow was sitting cross-legged with her elbows on her knees and her chin in her hands. Tears were trickling down her cheeks. She sniffled and said quietly, "Fox Tail was a good brother."

Two Knives nodded at her and at Dove Sings, and Dove Sings went to Bright Rainbow and draped an arm over the girl's shoulders to comfort her.

"Fox Tail was a good son, too."

Bright Rainbow looked up, her face gleaming wet. "Why did he have to die? It is not right."

"Death comes to all of us, little one," Dove Sings said. "We never know the day or the manner."

"But *why*?"

"You might as well ask why does the sun shine during the day and the moon rise at night. Death just is."

"I do not understand why it has to be."

Two Knives said, "There are many things in life that we do not understand. If we dwell on them, we will be sad. The important thing is to live the best we can and be as happy as we can and let the rest take care of itself."

Elk Running stopped pacing. "Listen!"

From the side of the lodge came a growl. The Devil Cat went on growling as it moved to the rear of the lodge and the growl faded.

"It has gone into the forest," Elk Running guessed. "We should go after it."

"You would not say that if you had seen it," Two Knives told him. "It is not like a normal cat."

They had enough firewood to last all night. They slept lying close to the flames, Dove Sings in Two Knives's arms, Bright Rainbow in hers. In the distance wolves wailed and coyotes crooned and once a brown bear roared, but their valley was still.

Two Knives did not sleep well. He would doze and wake with a start and then doze off again. This made two nights he had not gotten much sleep. Toward dawn he sat up, stiff and as tired as when he had lain down, and eased clear of Dove Sings and over to the hide. He took the lance. Quietly, he untied the hide enough to look out. It was too dark yet to see anything. He retied the hide and went back and waited for the others to rouse.

They had not slept well either. Dove Sings had shadows under her eyes. Bright Rainbow's eyes were red. Elk Running yawned and scratched and scowled at the world.

"I did not hear the cat all night, Father. It must be gone."

"We will go see," Two Knives said.

"Now?" Dove Sings said. "Why not wait until the sun is all the way up? That way it cannot take you by surprise."

"It took Fox Tail by surprise," Two Knives said, and was sorry he did when she flinched as if she had been struck. He strode to the flap. "I will go first."

"Be careful," Dove Sings said.

Chapter Six

In the gray light of predawn, the valley was serene and still save for writhing tendrils of mist.

Two Knives had slung his bow over his shoulder and was holding the lance as he edged around the lodge. Elk Running was behind him. Two Knives was careful to keep his back to the lodge and whispered to his son to do the same.

Two Knives stopped and probed the murky depths of the greenery for their adversary.

"Where is it?" Elk Running whispered.

Two Knives would like to think it was gone for good. But if the Devil Cat was like its tawny cousins, it had a territory it roamed. Which meant it would be back.

"Do you see it anywhere?"

"Not yet."

"I want to kill it for what it did to Fox Tail. I want to skin it and hang the hide on our wall."

To the east a golden glow was spreading across the sky. The stars were blinking out and being replaced by light blue.

Elk Running fidgeted. "How long will we stand here?"

"No longer," Two Knives said. He believed the Devil Cat was gone, if only for a while. Hurrying inside, he imparted the news to his wife and daughter, ending with "We should go while we can."

"Go where?" Dove Sings asked.

"We must leave the valley."

All three of them stared at him as if they must have misheard.

"We have lived here since before Fox Tail was born," Dove Sings said. "It is our home."

"We must go far enough that the Devil Cat will not find us," Two Knives said. "We can pack and be gone before the morning is done." They did not have a lot of possessions.

"We are running away?" Elk Running said.

"We are."

"It is wrong to run. This is our home, Father. And what of my brother? Did he die for nothing?"

"He died as a warning to us," Two Knives said. "The Devil Cat is too smart and too strong for us to kill. Our only hope to live is to let it have the valley."

"I do not like running."

"You are young yet. When you have grown more you will see that running to live another day is better than dying."

Dove Sings surprised him by saying, "I do not like running, either, husband. We should fight."

"For this?" Two Knives said, and stepping to the wall of limbs and brush, he smacked it. "We can build another lodge."

"I have many happy memories of our valley. We have been in peace here and our life has been good."

"Until now."

"I like it here, too," Bright Rainbow said.

Two Knives was irritated with them. He was the father and husband and they should accede to his wisdom. "The valley is not worth our lives."

"I think it is," Elk Running said.

"You have not seen the Devil Cat as I have," Two Knives told him. "You do now know what we face."

"It is an animal, and animals can be killed."

"So can we," Two Knives argued, but it was apparent he was speaking for nothing. The three were determined to stay. "My heart is sad that you oppose me."

"We do no such thing," Dove Sings said. "We only want to fight where you want to run."

"You think me a coward."

Dove Sings came over and clasped his hand. "You always put us above all else. I love that about you. But you must not let it make you weak when you must be strong."

Two Knives was stunned. She had never talked to him like this. "We fight and we might die."

"I have lived long with you. I would die happy with you at my side."

His head in a whirl, Two Knives sat by the fire. He needed to think. Every instinct he had warned against this folly. "Killing the Devil Cat will not be easy."

"We could set a snare," Elk Running said.

"We would need rope as thick as my arm."

"A pit, then?" Dove Sings suggested.

"It would take us half a moon to dig one big enough and deep enough," Two Knives noted.

Dove Sings hunkered beside him. "Here is an idea. We could go to the Shoshones and ask for help. Their leader, Touch the Clouds, has brought us deer meat."

"Once," Two Knives said. She made perfect sense, but a part of him balked at going to outsiders.

"What about Wolverine? He was nice. He would help."

"I would not know where to find him."

"How about that other white man? The one everyone says is a friend to all Indians. The one who took a Shoshone woman for his wife?"

"They call him Grizzly Killer," Two Knives said. "We have never met him. What reason would he have to help us?"

"Then it is us alone."

Elk Running said, "Three against one cat."

"Four," Bright Rainbow amended.

That made them smile. Dove Sings held her arms open and Bright Rainbow stepped into them and Dove Sings hugged her.

Elk Running patted his sister on the shoulder and said, "We would not forget you."

Two Knives racked his mind for a means of slaying a creature nearly impossible to slay. Poison would work if he could get the cat to eat tainted meat. A shallow pit lined with sharp stakes wouldn't kill it but might severely wound it and make it easy to track and finish off. So there were possibilities. The trick was to choose the best.

"I will make breakfast," Dove Sings announced, and moved to the parfleche in which she stored their dried meat and pemmican and roots.

Two Knives wasn't hungry; he was too on edge. But it would be good for her to keep busy, so he rubbed his belly and said, "I could eat a bull elk." He had another idea: rigging the lance to impale the cat. With the right bait and a sapling, it could be done.

"Where did the Devil Cat come from?" Elk Running wondered. "It has not bothered us before."

"The old ones say a Devil Cat is born into the world every hundred winters," Two Knives said. "It is as rare as a white buffalo. But where the white buffalo brings good medicine, the Devil Cat is an omen for evil."

"Father?" Bright Rainbow said softly.

"I would like to see a white buffalo one day," Elk Running said. "Didn't Grandfather see one?"

"Father?" Bright Rainbow said again.

"Yes, he did," Two Knives confirmed. "On the prairie when he was about your age."

"Father!"

"What is it, little one?"

Bright Rainbow pointed.

Two Knives looked, and his breath caught in his throat. He had forgotten to tie the hide when he came back in and there was the Devil Cat, the hide pushed back, crouched in the opening and glaring at them with slanted eyes of blazing yellow-green fire.

"No!" Dove Sings shouted, and scooped Rainbow into her arms.

Elk Running had set down his bow, but he had a knife in a sheath on his hip. Drawing it, he leaped at the giant.

"Stop!" Two Knives shouted, too late, for the next instant the Devil Cat reared and struck Elk Running across the chest. Elk Running cried out and was flung at Two Knives. Both of them went down and the lance was knocked from Two Knives's grasp.

Two Knives sought to rise and defend his family. Out of the corner of his eye he glimpsed a black blur. Dove Sings screamed. He pushed from under

Elk Running, who was thrashing and spurting scarlet, and rose.

Dove Sings was down. The Devil Cat had her by the throat. She was striking its head and neck to no avail as its fangs ravaged her flesh.

Two Knives scooped up the lance. He thrust at the Devil Cat's side, but it was too fast and dodged. He went after it and it skipped away. He had never seen anything so fast. Feinting left, he speared to the right and the tip penetrated the cat's shoulder.

There was not a lot of room for the Devil Cat to move, but move it did, vaulting clear.

Dove Sings was struggling to rise. Her throat and the front of her dress were red. She saw Two Knives and reached for him and would have buckled had he not wrapped an arm around her waist.

"I have you."

The Devil Cat was crouched on the far side, hissing mightily, its long tail flicking back and forth.

"We must flee," Dove Sings gurgled.

Two Knives turned to his son. Elk Running's eyes were wide and his face wooden. A crimson pool was spreading under the boy's body. Whirling, Two Knives propelled his wife toward the hide. He looked for Bright Rainbow but didn't see her. Another moment and he burst out into the harsh glare of the hot sun. He turned to the right, or tried to. The hide exploded outward and the Devil Cat was on them. It leaped full onto Dove Sings, ripping her from his grasp and smashing her belly-down on the ground. Their eyes met and she raised her fingers to Two Knives in mute appeal. He went to throw himself at the cat—and the beast bit down on the top of her head. Its fangs punctured her skull as his flint knives would puncture melons. He saw the life fly from her, saw her eyes go empty.

In a rage, the Devil Cat shook her and clawed at her body.

Nearly numb with a hurt that surpassed any physical wound, Two Knives ran. He didn't know where he was running. All he could think of was that his wife was gone. He had gone a dozen strides when he remembered his daughter. "Bright Rainbow!" he cried, and stopped and turned. He took a step to rush back and heard her call him.

"Father!"

Bright Rainbow stepped from behind a nearby pine. Sweeping her into his arms, Two Knives fled. He did not care if some would call him a coward. He had lost three of those he loved; he would not lose Bright Rainbow or his own life if he could help it. He realized he still had the spear and firmed his grip.

"Mother," Bright Rainbow said, and sobbed.

"Not yet, little one," Two Knives cautioned between puffs for breath. "We must be as quiet as we can or the Devil Cat will be after us." He glanced back, but there was no sign of it.

"I am sorry, Father," Bright Rainbow said, sniffling. She wiped at her face with her sleeve. "I will try."

The woods were a green tangle. Two Knives had been through them countless times and knew them well, yet he couldn't tell where he was or which direction he was running. A glance at the sun revealed he was headed north. He remembered a certain slope and a possible haven, and he ran faster.

"They are both dead, aren't they?" Bright Rainbow asked.

"Yes."

"What will we do without Mother?"

"Quiet." But Two Knives wondered the same thing: what *would* he do without the woman who had been everything to him? Sorrow washed over him, but he fought it. As he had told Bright Rainbow, now was not the time. There would be ample time later on for grief—provided they lived.

Branches loomed in their path. Thickets rose in impassable barriers. Logs and boulders had to be vaulted or avoided. At one point Two Knives nearly tripped over the spear and shifted his grip so he held it higher and it wouldn't happen again.

"Where are we going?" Bright Rainbow asked.

"I said no talking." Two Knives was listening for pursuit. The Devil Cat was bound to come after them. It had killed everyone else. Which proved that its reputation for bloodlust was well deserved.

"Father," Bright Rainbow said.

"Not now." Two Knives had spied his goal.

"Father, please."

"We are almost there." Two Knives weaved through oaks. Above him canted a bluff. Midway up was a jumble of rocks from a bygone slide and above it their salvation.

"It is important."

Two Knives remembered not listening to her in the lodge, and the tragic consequences. "What is it, little one?"

"The Devil Cat is after us."

Two Knives glanced over his shoulder. "No!" he cried, and pumped his legs. He reached the slope and up they flew, small stones and dirt sliding out from under his feet. In desperation he lunged the final distance and hurled his daughter from him. Turning, he held the lance ready to thrust.

A black streak was almost to the edge of the forest.

"What do I do?" Bright Rainbow wailed.

"There!" Two Knives yelled, and nodded at what he hoped would be their sanctuary.

"What about you?"

"Do it!"

Then there was no time for talking. There was no time for anything.

The Devil Cat was on them.

Part Three

The Call of the Heart

Chapter Seven

Evelyn King was in love. It had taken a while for her to admit it, but now that she had, she was giddy with glee. Which was strange, since until recently the last thing on her mind was boys. Now one in particular was all she ever thought about, or dreamed about, or imagined going on long rides with in the mountains or on long walks around the lake or simply sitting and staring into his eyes. She giggled and caught herself.

"What is happening to me?" Evelyn asked out loud, and shook her head in amusement. She was changing. Her mother had always said the day would come when she would go from being a girl to being a woman, and she'd always scoffed. Maybe it happened to other females; it wasn't going to happen to her.

Evelyn had doubted she would ever fall in love. She had doubted she would ever marry and have a family. So what if her mother and most other women since the dawn of creation had done it? But once again her mother had been proven to be right.

Now that Evelyn thought about it, her parents had been right about a lot of things. It made her wonder what other notions she held that she was wrong about. It frazzled a person, being mistaken like that.

Life sure was strange, Evelyn reflected. There she'd been, a perfectly content sixteen-year-old girl, happy with her life and with no hankering to change it, and life went and threw a surprise at her. Life went and kindled a flame that she couldn't quench if she wanted to, and she didn't want to.

Evelyn smiled at her reflection in the lake. "Who would have thought it?" she asked out loud. Certainly not her. She'd had no interest in boys. None whatsoever.

She resumed her stroll around the lake shore toward her parents' cabin. Around her the valley was vibrant with life. King Valley, it was called, named after her father. By the calendar it was early autumn, but you wouldn't know it from the hot weather. Indian Summer, folks back East would say. A last heat wave before the weather turned chill and the oaks and the aspens changed color.

Someone was coming toward her, a man with a mane of white hair and a warm smile. Like her father, he wore buckskins and was armed with a Hawken rifle and a brace of pistols. She returned his smile with affection.

"Forsooth, fair maiden! Don't you look pretty in your new dress and bonnet!"

"Uncle Shakespeare," Evelyn said. He wasn't really her uncle, but he had been his father's best friend since before she was born and she had known him since she could remember. "What are you up to today?"

Shakespeare McNair stopped and placed the stock of his rifle on the ground and leaned on the barrel. "I paid your father a visit to needle him."

"What about?"

"Anything and everything. I like to bring color to his cheeks."

"You are the biggest tease I know. Ma says if a person could make a living at teasing, you could have stayed back in the States and been rich."

Shakespeare stiffened in mock indignation and quoted the Bard he was named after. "'O serpent heart, hid with a flowery face. Did ever dragon keep so fair a cave?'"

"Now, now," Evelyn chided. "She was only saying."

"That's the trouble with females," Shakespeare grumped. "They are forever using their tongues as rapiers and piercing us poor men to the quick."

"You men deserve it."

"Since when? What do we do that you women delight in pricking us so?"

"It's how you are."

Shakespeare sniffed and quoted, "'You do unbend your noble strength, to think so brainsickly of things.'"

Evelyn laughed. "Is that even a word? Brainsickly? Sometimes I think that William S., as you like to call him, just made up words to suit him."

Shakespeare's indignation became genuine. "Why, you upstart. I'll have you know he was the greatest word-weaver who ever drew breath. He made poetry of the plain and showed the real and the true of all that is."

"Oh, really?" Evelyn said. "What about that silly play of his with the fairies and Cupid?"

Shakespeare made a sound remarkably similar to a goose being throttled. "Did my ears deceive me, child? Did you just call the Bard *silly*?" He quoted again. "'Is there no military policy how virgins might blow up men?'"

Evelyn gave a mild start. "What did you just say?"

"That you have besmirched the greatest writer of all time."

"No. That other thing."

"Oh. You mean about virgins?" A sly smile curled McNair's seamed features. "That reminds me. How is the handsome Romeo these days? Rumor has it that the two of you are glued at the elbow." He chortled merrily and said, "Glued at the elbow! I do make myself laugh, if I say so myself."

"That will be enough of that."

"Oh ho?" Shakespeare returned. "The young maiden can dish it out, but she can't take it?"

"You shouldn't poke fun at something like that."

"Like what? Love?"

Evelyn was growing annoyed. She cared for Shakespeare dearly, but he had a knack for getting a rise out of people. "I never said I was in love."

"You never said you weren't. Not that anyone would believe you if you did. The proof of the pudding is in the tasting, young one."

"Meaning what, exactly?"

"Meaning if it waddles like a duck and quacks like a duck, it won't do any good to call it a moose."

Evelyn put her hands on her hips. "I've heard that people your age tend to babble a lot and I reckon it must be true."

"Here, now," Shakespeare said. "Pick on anything you want but my years. I have earned these wrinkles honorably." He glanced behind him and then gazed past her and came closer and lowered his voice. "How are the two of you doing, by the way? Has Horatio said anything about Dega and you?"

"Horatio," as Evelyn well knew, was Shakespeare's

nickname for her father. "What would Pa have to say about what I do? It's between Dega and me."

"Does your father mind the two of you being together? Sometimes parents take exception."

"I don't see how he could," Evelyn said. "So what if I'm white and Dega is an Indian? Pa married a Shoshone, after all."

"That wasn't what I was talking about," Shakespeare clarified. "Land sakes, girl, I married a sassy red wench myself."

"Oh, Uncle Shakespeare."

"Don't 'Uncle Shakespeare' me. I will call my wife that to her face and she will be flattered."

"So Blue Water Woman is a wench, is she?"

"All women are. Some hide it better than others, but deep down all women want the same thing."

"And what would that be?"

Shakespeare started to say something and caught himself. Instead he smiled and said, "They want a heart to entwine with their own."

Evelyn thought of Dega and her chest grew warm. "Even if that's true, I'm still not admitting I'm in love."

"A woman's prerogative. And for your sake I will graciously drop the subject."

"Thank you," Evelyn said. "I'll have to tell your wife that she's wrong about you."

"What did the wretch say?"

Evelyn snorted. "How did she go from being a wench to a wretch?"

"She's female. Your kind does it with every other breath."

"Oh, Uncle Shakespeare."

"Don't start with that again. What did my darling wife claim this time?"

"Only that your tongue is so tart, you must have been born with a sour disposition. But she was smiling when she said it."

"That was the word she used? Tart?"

Evelyn nodded. "She was quite proud of it. She said it was a word worthy of your precious William S."

"The nerve," Shakespeare said, and paraphrased, "All that is within her does condemn itself for being there." Lifting his rifle, he marched on by. "If you'll excuse me, there's a certain upstart who needs a tongue-lashing."

Evelyn grinned and continued on her way. She thought of his remark about the military and virgins and felt herself blush. That was another thing she'd never given any attention until recently. Why should she, when she was never going to marry? Sighing, she stopped and gazed toward the east end of the lake. The Nansusequa lodge was a dark block in the shadows of the tall trees. Dega was there somewhere, going about his daily chores. It had been a few days since she saw him and she dearly yearned to.

That got her thinking. Usually when they were together, others were around. His family or her family or Shakespeare and his wife. It was rare for them to be alone. The last time had been when they went on a long ride up into the mountains. She decided to go on another. Only she couldn't just tell her mother and father and say she wanted to go off with Dega to be alone with him. She needed an excuse.

Over by the cabin the chickens were pecking and taking dirt baths. The rooster flapped his wings at her as she went by. She opened the door and went in and stood a moment so her eyes could adjust. Her mother, Winona, was at the counter chopping a rabbit into bits for a stew.

"Where's Pa?" Evelyn asked.

"He went to visit your brother and see how Louisa is coming along," Winona said in her impeccable English.

Evelyn pulled out a chair and sat at the table. Her sister-in-law was in the family way and everyone was doting over her. She wondered if they would do the same when she was in the family way, and blushed again.

"How was your walk?"

"It's a beautiful day," Evelyn said.

Winona turned. She had a bloody knife in one hand, and the fingers of her other hand dripped red drops. "Too beautiful to clean your room as you promised you would?"

"I said I would get it done by suppertime."

"And you will stall until it is nearly time to eat and then do it," Winona predicted.

Evelyn wanted to stay on her mother's good side, so she said, "I'll clean it in a few minutes. First I wanted to ask you something."

Winona turned back to the counter and began putting the pieces and bits into a pot. "I am listening."

"Pretty soon the weather will change," Evelyn began by a devious route. "Winter will be here and we'll have snow up to our necks."

"Sometimes the snow is deep, yes. Do you want your father to repair that sled he made you?"

"What? No. I haven't used that in years." Evelyn traced the shape of a heart on the tabletop.

"Then what was your point?"

"Only that once the snow hits, we don't get to go anywhere. We can be socked in for days or even weeks."

"Winter is as it is."

"I know that. I'm not griping about the snow. I'm saying that I'd like to get away for a day. Maybe ride up into the high country."

Winona shifted toward her. "Oh?"

"Yes." Evelyn saw the hint of a grin at the corners of her mother's mouth. Or maybe it was her imagination.

"Would you go alone?"

"No. Pa and you wouldn't like that. So I was thinking of asking Dega to go along. I was thinking we could pack food and make a picnic of it. The last outing of the summer, so to speak."

"So to speak," Winona repeated, and stabbed a juicy chunk. "It is fine by me if it is fine by your father."

Inwardly, Evelyn smiled. Her father nearly always let her do things if she got her mother's approval first. "I'll ask him when he gets back."

"Have you asked Dega yet?"

"No. If Pa says yes, I'll ride over to the Nansusequa lodge later. We could go tomorrow morning and be back by nightfall."

"All day? That is a long picnic." Winona looked at her. "What will you do with yourselves?"

"Mostly we'll ride and eat and admire the scenery and the animals," Evelyn said, her cheeks warm yet again.

"You will go armed. Take your rifle and your pistols. And you will tell Dega to be on his guard at all times."

"We're not kids," Evelyn said.

"You're not adults, either." Winona put down the butcher knife. She poured water from a pitcher into the pot and carried the pot and a large wooden spoon to the stove. "After all the things that have happened to you, you shouldn't take the wilderness lightly."

"That's one thing I'll never do," Evelyn vowed. Over the years she had encountered bears and wolves and hostiles and more, and nearly lost her life on several occasions.

"I hope Dega's parents will let him."

"Why wouldn't they?" Evelyn asked. "They've always been as nice as can be to me."

"I am sure they will," Winona said. "They are dear people and have become good friends. We are lucky to have them as neighbors."

"Yes," Evelyn agreed. "We are."

"You will be back by nightfall without fail?"

"I give you my word, Ma," Evelyn said, averting her gaze. She couldn't look her mother in the eye after telling such a bold-faced lie. She had no intention of making it back by dark. In fact, she planned on the opposite; she was going to stay all night alone with Dega in the wilderness.

She couldn't wait.

Chapter Eight

Tihikanima found her son seated on a log in a sunlit glade. He was sitting so still and blended in so well, with his green buckskins, she almost didn't spot him. He was gazing off toward King Lake with a longing expression she had seen many times of late. He wasn't really looking at the lake; he was pining for the new female in his life. She strolled out of the trees, her arms crossed over her bosom, her doeskin dress the same shade of green as his. He was so enrapt, he didn't notice her until she was almost on top of him.

"Mother!" Degamawaku stood. "What brings you here?"

"I was out for a walk," Tihi lied. She had come specifically to see him, but he must not know that. "May I join you?"

"Of course." Dega motioned at the log. "There is plenty of room for both of us."

"What were you thinking about when I came up?" Tihi reminded herself that she must not be obvious or he would resent it.

"About a buck I saw this morning," Dega said.

"Does this buck have a name?" Tihi countered. "And would the name be Evelyn King?"

Dega smiled and sat next to her. "I do not think of her all the time."

"Only most of it."

"I have made no secret of my fondness for her. She is a fine girl, Evelyn."

"Yes, she is," Tihi was quick to agree. In that, at least, she was sincere. She did think that Evelyn was a fine person: cheerful and courteous and caring. But to Tihi that wasn't enough.

Out on the water, mallards were swimming and geese were honking. A large fish leaped clear and splashed down.

"What are you intentions with her?" Tihi asked. She had to force herself to keep her tone unemotional.

Dega shifted. "Why do you ask?"

"You are my son," Tihi said. "You are my oldest. I have nurtured you from when you were a baby in a cradleboard. I care for you and want only the best for you."

"Did Father send you to talk to me about her?" Dega asked.

"I am here on my own," Tihi admitted. Her husband would be upset if he knew. She had broached the subject with him and he had made it plain that he did not want her to interfere. But she couldn't stand by and say nothing. Too much was at stake.

"I should think you would be happy if Evelyn and I become close," Dega said. "I could do worse than pick her as my wife."

There it was, out in the open where Tihi wanted it. Now she must be extra careful. "You are young yet to think of that."

"I have seen almost nineteen summers."

"Evelyn has seen only sixteen."

"So?" Dega said. "You took Father as your husband when you were that age. And Evelyn tells me that among her people many take husbands and wives when they are as young as she and I are."

"Among her people," Tihi repeated. He had unwittingly given her the opening she wanted.

"Why do you say it like that?"

"She is white and you are not."

"So?" Dega said again. "Nate King is married to Winona, a Shoshone. Shakespeare McNair is married to Blue Water Woman, a Flathead. Zach King is half and half, and he has a white wife. What difference does it make that Evelyn looks white and I do not?"

Tihi chose her next words with great care. She didn't want him angry with her. He must think she shared his fondness for Evelyn, even if she didn't. "When two hearts are in love, only their love matters."

"That is how I feel, too."

"But there is more than just your hearts involved, my son. She is white. You are Nansusequa." Tihi paused. "Need I mention that our family is all that is left of our people? That the rest of our people were wiped out by whites who sought our land for themselves?"

"I was there, Mother," Dega said bitterly. "It was the most terrible day of my life. I do not understand why Manitoa deserted us."

To the Nansusequa, Manitoa was the source of all that was. Their other name for it meant That Which Was In All Things. They revered the Manitoa above all else. Because of that reverence, for untold generations they had striven to live in harmony with all that was around them, and by doing so, be close to That Which Was In All Things. For untold generations they were a peaceful people devoted to one another and their customs. Then, in one brief burst of brutal violence, all that they were and all that they believed had been nearly wiped out by greedy whites.

Only their family escaped. The five of them were the last of their kind, the very last of the Nansusequas.

"Did Manitoa desert us or did we desert Manitoa?" Tihi responded. She'd had a hard time reconciling the tragedy herself. She could still hear the screams and see warriors and women she had known all her life having their brains blown out or their bodies skewered on sharp blades. "But it is not That Which Is In All Things that I have come to talk about."

"Then what?"

"Our responsibility to those we lost."

Dega scratched his handsome head in puzzlement. "I am confused," he confessed.

"As the last of our kind, we owe it to those who fell to live as Nansusequa should."

"We do that," Dega said.

"We wear Nansusequa clothes and live in a Nansusequa lodge," Tihi said. "But what about in here?" She touched her head. "Or in here?" She touched her bosom over her heart.

"We are Nansusequa through and through, as the whites would say," Dega declared.

"Are we?" Tihi paused for effect, then said, "A Nansusequa does not give his heart to an outsider. Nansusequas only marry Nansusequas." There. She had said it.

Dega stared at her for the longest while, his face impossible to read. Finally he said, "I cannot believe what I am hearing."

"Why not?"

"You are saying that you do not want me to feel for Evelyn as I do. You are saying that you do not want the two of us to be together."

"She is an outsider."

"The Kings are our friends," Dega said. "They helped us when no one else would. They gave us a place to live."

"Nate and Winona do not hate our kind, I will grant them that," Tihi conceded. "But as friendly as they have been, they are not Nansusequa. As generous as they have been, they are not Nansusequa."

"It makes no difference to me."

"It should," Tihi said. "If you love your people, if you mourn for them every day as I do, then you should want to honor their memory by not giving up their ways."

"You have thought this all this time?"

Yes, Tihi had, but her husband insisted she not interfere, and until now she had abided by his wishes. "I did not have cause to think about it until you took up with her."

"I care for Evelyn greatly, Mother."

To soften the sting, Tihi smiled and ran her hand over his long black hair and caressed his cheek. "I know that, son. It is why I have been reluctant to bring it up. The last thing I ever want to do is hurt your feelings."

"I care for her greatly," Dega reiterated.

"Enough to take her for your wife. When will that be?"

"I . . ." Dega hesitated. "I have not thought that far ahead."

Tihi felt a twinge of anger. Not at him, at Evelyn King. For he was plainly lying to protect Evelyn, and she could count the number of times that he had lied to her on one hand and have fingers left. "Let us talk that far ahead, if you do not mind."

"I always do as you say," Dega said, but he did not sound happy about it.

Tihi's anger climbed, but she kept her self-control. "Let us say that Evelyn and you continue to see each other. Let us say there comes a time when you think that you love her and she thinks that she loves you."

"It will not be because we *think* it," Dega said. "It will be because we *are* in love."

"Of course. My mistake. And when that time comes, you will naturally want her to be yours and she will naturally want you to be hers. So let us say that you become husband and wife. What then?"

Dega appeared puzzled. "We would live as Father and you do."

"Will you come live with us?"

"What?"

"You heard me," Tihi said. "It is Nansuseqea custom for a man to bring his new wife to live in the lodge of his father and mother. If you take Evelyn King for your wife, will she come live in our lodge?"

"I do not know if she would like that."

"Have you asked her?"

"No."

"Why not?"

"It has not come up."

"All right. Let us put that aside for the moment." Tihi went on smiling to show her forbearance. "One day you will have children. How will you raise them?"

"As Father and you raised me."

"As Nansusequas? Or as white? Evelyn's mother

is Shoshone, but Evelyn prefers white ways to Shoshone ways."

"I hadn't thought of that," Dega said.

"You should. How your children will be brought
up is important. Will you raise them as whites so
they never know their Nansusequa heritage? Or will
you raise them as your father and I raised you and
your sisters, as true People of the Forest?"

Dega put his elbows on his knees and his chin his
hands. "There is more to marrying her than I imagined."

"I am happy you see that. It is why I brought it
up." Tihi shammed interest in a bald eagle soaring
above distant peaks. "We are the last of our kind, my
son. Once we are gone, the Nansusequa are gone.
Unless . . ." She rubbed his shoulder. "Unless you
and your sisters raise your children in the Nansusequa way, and their children after them."

"Speak plainly, Mother. Are you against me marrying Evelyn?"

"Did I say that?" Tihi hoped she was hiding her
emotions well enough. "Should you decide she
should be your wife, I will stand by you as I have
always stood by you in all that you have done. But it
would be a shame, would it not, to have the Nansusequa way be lost to the world?"

"Yes, it would."

Tihikanima smiled sweetly. Now she must feed
the fire of doubt she had planted so it became a rag-
ing bonfire. "Think about it, my son. We are the last
of our kind. I keep saying that because it is important for you to fully understand. After we are gone,
the Nansusequa will be no more." She paused and
gently squeezed his arm. "Unless you and your sis-

ters carry on the beliefs and customs of our people. On your shoulders rests whether the Nansusequa die out or are reborn."

"Reborn?" Dega repeated.

"Your children, my son, and Tenikawaku's and Mikikawaku's, are our future. They will in turn have children of their own, and their children after them. Hopefully, large families. If each of you has five children and each of them has five children and so on, in a hundred summers there will be a hundred Nansusequa where now there are only five."

"I had not thought of that, either."

"Do you see how important it is? In your hands rests the rebuilding of our people. In your hands is the future of all that we are."

Dega gazed off toward the lake, and a troubled look came over him. "In our hands," he said softly.

Tihi pressed her argument. "They *must* be raised as Nansusequa. Not in any other way. Certainly not as whites. They will not be Nansusequa then. Do you see that?"

"Yes."

Tihi patted his shoulder. "Good. I was worried that perhaps you did not, which is why I brought all this up."

"Have you talked to my sisters about it?"

"I have talked to Teni. She is of the age where she might take a husband if she finds one who suits her. Miki is young yet. I will wait until she is a little older."

"You have given me much to think about."

Tihi decided to give him more. "Think of how different we are from the whites. We believe in living in harmony with all that is. The whites believe they must control all that is and bend it to their will. We believe in That Which Is In All Things and respect the right of all living things to the gift of life the Manitoa has bestowed. To us, our fellow creatures are our brothers and sisters. The deer in the woods. The elk in the thick brush. The birds in the trees. To the whites they are nothing but animals. Beasts, they call them, and slaughter them for furs and for food. Is this not true?"

Dega said reluctantly, "With most whites it is."

"I ask you. Does Evelyn King believe in the Manitoa as we do?"

"No."

"Does she regard the deer and the elk as her brothers and sisters, or does she regard them as animals?"

"To her they are animals," Dega said, with an odd rasping to his voice.

"Does she give thanks each day to That Which Is In All Things for the breath of life in her, or does she take that breath for granted?"

Dega sadly stared at the ground.

"I have spoken enough for now." Tihi stood and caressed his head. "Ponder my words and you will agree. You must take for your wife a woman who will live the Nansusequa way. No other will do. Do you agree?"

Barely audible, Dega said, "Yes, Mother."

"Good. I am sorry if this has upset you."

"No. You did right."

"Thank you." Tihi smiled and walked off. When she was out of his hearing she declared, "So much for Evelyn King."

Tihikanima laughed.

Chapter Nine

The bright afternoon sun bathed the deep blue of King Lake.

Evelyn slowed her horse from a trot to a walk as she neared the east end. She was always so eager to see Degamawaku that she yearned to rush into his arms. But that would be unseemly. So she walked Buttercup up to the Great Lodge in the shade of the tall trees and dismounted. No one was about. She walked toward the opening and stopped short when Dega's father emerged. "Hello, Wakumassee," she said.

Waku was dressed all in green. He had a broad chest and a high forehead and always carried himself straight and tall. Smiling warmly, he clasped her hand. "Evelyn King." His English was thickly accented. He was trying hard to learn the language and doing the best of all of them, Dega included. "My heart very happy to see you."

"I came to talk to Dega."

"He not here," Waku told her. "He went walk a while ago and not back yet."

"Oh." Evelyn tried to hide her disappointment. "Do you know which way he went?"

"I not notice. Sorry." Waku gestured at the Great Lodge. "Want come in? We have tea your mother give us."

"No, thank you." Evelyn was only interested in

seeing Dega. She scanned the woods and spied a figure approaching. "There's Tihikanima. Maybe she knows where he is."

Tihikanima came out of the trees. On seeing Evelyn she spread her arms wide and smiled and embraced her.

"How do you do?" Evelyn said politely. The mother was always friendly to her, but for some reason Evelyn never felt entirely comfortable around her.

Tihikanima spoke to Wakumassee and he translated.

"My wife say she much happy to see you. She say you like daughter to her. Always welcome."

"Thank her for me," Evelyn requested, "and please ask her if she has seen Dega."

Waku translated, then said, "My wife say she not see our son. She say him maybe not back until dark."

"Oh." This time Evelyn let her disappointment show. "I was hoping to talk to him. I want to ask him to go on a picnic with me tomorrow."

"What is picnic?" Waku asked.

"We would take food in a basket and go for a ride," Evelyn explained. "Find a good spot and eat it." She refrained from mentioning that secretly she hoped to keep him out overnight.

"That sound nice." Again Waku translated for the benefit of his wife. "Tihi say we tell Dega when him come back."

"Thank her for me." It struck Evelyn that the mother hardly ever spoke English or even tried to, and she wondered why that was. She turned and climbed on Buttercup. "My ma wanted me to remind you that your family is invited to Sunday supper."

"We be there," Waku assured her. "Thank mother."

"I will." Evelyn rode to the south along the shore. She was glum. Putting off the picnic another day or two really made no difference except that she'd had her heart set on doing it the next day. She gave her Hawken an angry shake.

Ahead, several does were drinking. They raised their heads and pricked their ears, then bounded off with their tails erect.

A large snake slithered in among a cluster of rocks. Evelyn only caught a glimpse and couldn't tell what kind it was. To be safe, she reined wide to avoid it. They'd had problems with rattlesnakes recently and she'd fought shy of snakes ever since. She was near the edge of the woods and instinctively raised her rifle when a shadow moved.

"How you be, Evelyn?"

Her heart bursting for joy, Evelyn drew rein. "Dega!" she exclaimed happily, and vaulted down. She ran to him and went to throw her arms around him and then glanced back at the Great Lodge and the figures standing in front of it, and stepped back. "How are you?"

"I fine," Dega said.

Something in his tone suggested otherwise. Evelyn wanted to take his hand, but his parents might see. "I just talked to your ma and pa. They told me you had gone for a walk."

"I thinking of you."

Evelyn grinned in delight. "I can't stop thinking of you, either. Last night I could hardly sleep, I wanted to be with you so much." She glanced toward the lodge again and turned her back to it. "Why don't we walk a little ways? I have an idea you might like."

Dega fell into step beside her. "It pretty day."

"Yes, it is."

"Nansusequa thank Manitoa for pretty days," Dega said, plainly struggling with his English.

"That's nice." Evelyn didn't understand why he was bringing it up.

"Who whites thank?"

Evelyn's puzzlement grew. "We've talked about this before. What you call Manitoa, whites call God Almighty. Whites give thanks to him for everything."

"Manitoa and God not same."

"They are close enough." Evelyn sidled closer so their shoulders brushed as they walked. "Why talk about that when I want to talk about us? Wouldn't it be great if we could get away for a spell by ourselves?"

"Get away?"

"Go off alone. Just the two of us." Evelyn stopped and faced him and looked into his eyes. "What do you say? I'd like for us to go on a picnic. I'll pack the food so all you have to bring is yourself. We can leave tomorrow, early. I'll tell my folks that we'll be back by dark, but if we're not, well . . ." She grinned and shrugged.

"What is pic-nic?"

"I just told you. It's where you take food off into the wilds and eat and talk and things. Wouldn't you like that? You and me and no one else?"

"Where we go?" Dega asked. "Somewhere in valley?"

"Oh no." Evelyn lowered her voice as if others could overhear. "This valley is big, sure, but we never know when my brother or Shakespeare or somebody might come along. So I was thinking we should go where no one else would bother us."

"Where that be?"

Evelyn lowered her voice even more. "Do you remember a while ago when we found a pass up on that mountain to the north?"

"How I forget?" Dega replied. "We meet bad men who try kill us."

"My pa and my brother took care of them. We'll be safe if we keep our eyes skinned." Evelyn touched his hand. "Pa and Uncle Shakespeare were going to close the pass with black powder, but they never got around to it. If we go through to the other side, no one will disturb us."

"That is far for pic-nic."

"Maybe so. But it's worth it for the privacy." Evelyn touched both his hands. "What do you say? Would you like to go? We can talk and eat and have a lot of fun."

"I would like talk," Dega said.

"Then it's settled." Impulsively, Evelyn rose onto the tips of her toes and kissed him on the cheek.

"I must tell Father and Mother. Maybe they not want me go."

"Why wouldn't they?" Evelyn asked. "They've let us go riding before. Besides, I mentioned it to them and they didn't say they minded."

"You tell them we maybe not back by night?"

"It didn't come up."

"Not good to keep"—Dega scrunched up his face as he searched for the right word—"secret."

"It's not as if we're lying to them. If anything, we might be fibbing, and a little fibbing never hurt anyone."

"I not understand. Lie is lie."

"Do you want to be with me or not?"

"I want you very much, yes."

"Then quit nit-picking. Be at my pa's cabin as soon after sunrise as you can. I'll be ready and waiting." Evelyn wanted to kiss him again but restrained herself. "It will be wonderful. You and me and no one else. Just as if we were married."

"Married," Dega said.

"Don't look so panicked. It's not as if I'm proposing." Evelyn laughed and turned. "You have made me the happiest girl alive."

"I have?"

"Dega, I feel . . ." Evelyn stopped and shook her head. "No. I'll save it for when we're alone."

"Save what?"

"We have some serious talking to do."

"Yes," Dega said. "We do."

Evelyn climbed on. "Remember. As early as you can so we make it over the pass by ten or so and have the rest of the day to ourselves."

"I be early," Dega promised.

Evelyn used her heels on Buttercup. She barely noticed her surroundings; she was floating on inner clouds of joy. Her plan was working.

Several geese honked, bringing Evelyn out of herself. A hawk was flying over the lake, and its shadow had caused them alarm. "Silly things," she said to herself. She remembered her father saying that he intended to shoot a goose before the weather turned cold, and her mouth watered. She liked goose and duck meat almost as much as mountain lion, which was her favorite. She'd balked the first time a plate of painter meat was put in front of her, but that first forkful changed her mind. It was delicious.

Smoke was rising from the McNairs' chimney. Evelyn half expected Shakespeare or Blue Water Woman to hear her horse and come out, but their door stayed closed.

Pale patches high on the cliffs to the west caught her eye. Mountain sheep, she reckoned. She had seen them up close a few times when she was younger and marveled at how they scaled sheer cliffs with the greatest of surefooted ease.

All the horses save hers were in the corral. She stripped off her saddle and draped it over the top rail and made sure to close the gate behind her or her father would have a fit. Whistling to herself, she strolled inside. Her mother was at the counter, chopping carrots. Her father was the table, reading one of his many books. She greeted them while propping her Hawken against the wall.

"Your mother tells me you'd like to go on a picnic tomorrow."

"It's all set," Evelyn said.

Nate King put down the book. "I want you to be careful, little one."

"I'm not so little anymore," Evelyn responded. It annoyed her that he couldn't seem to accept the fact that she was practically a grown woman. She went to the table and sat across from him. "Have you seen sign of any hostiles or beasts I should know about?"

"No. It's been peaceful."

Winona looked up from her carrots. "That is what worries him. He is always waiting, as the whites say, for the other shoe to drop."

"A person can't be too cautious in the wilderness," Nate said. "Not if he wants to go on breathing."

"We're only going on a picnic," Evelyn said.

"Tell that to the griz that stumbles across you. Or the war party out to count coup."

"You killed the last grizzly in our valley," Evelyn reminded him, "and the hostile tribes mostly leave us be."

"I had to kill the griz. It was trying to kill me," Nate said. "And the Blackfoot Confederacy and others leave us be because they don't know where we are."

"I'll be careful," Evelyn promised.

"I want you back by nightfall."

Evelyn smoothed her dress and flicked a speck of dust from her sleeve.

"Did you hear me, daughter?"

"Yes, Pa."

Nate grunted and returned to his book.

Evelyn was amazed at her audacity. Here she was, outright lying to her father. There was a time, not that long ago, when she wouldn't think of doing such a thing.

"Care to help me?" Winona asked from the counter. "We need potatoes peeled and cut."

"Sure," Evelyn said. She fetched the potato sack from the pantry and carried it in both hands to the counter. From a drawer she took a wood-handled knife with a narrow curved blade, and set to work. She had peeled potatoes so many times she could do it with her eyes shut. It gave her time to think about the morrow and Degamawaku.

"Are you here, daughter, or up in the sky with the birds?" Winona asked good-naturedly.

"I'm standing right next to you."

"The look in your eyes tells me your body is here but the rest of you is somewhere else."

"Can't a person think around here without being pestered?" Evelyn said sharply.

Winona stopped chopping carrots and turned. Nate put down his book and shifted in his chair.

"Is that any way to talk to your mother?"

"I'm sorry, Pa," Evelyn said quickly.

"I'm not the one you snapped at."

"I'm sorry, Ma. I don't know what got into me." Evelyn set down the knife and the potato and quickly crossed to the front door and stepped out into the glare of the hot sun. She walked toward the lake, scattering chickens in her path, and came to the water's edge. Clasping her hands so hard her knuckles hurt, she pretended not to notice when her shadow became two.

"Would you like to talk about it?" Winona asked.

"There's nothing to talk about."

"Something is bothering you. I would like to soothe your spirit so you are yourself again."

"There's nothing," Evelyn insisted.

"Did you see nothing when you went over to visit the Nansusequas?" Winona asked.

Evelyn stared out over the rippling surface of the water. Part of her wanted to stay silent, but another part recalled how caring and considerate her mother had always been, and she softened. "I feel things I've never felt before."

Winona ran a hand down the blue beads that adorned her doeskin dress. "All women go through what you are going through."

"That doesn't make it easier."

"No, it does not. One day you are a girl, the next you are a woman. One day you are playing with dolls, the next you think only of *them*. I remember how it was when I met your father. Until he came into my life, I did not give men much thought. Then something happened inside me and I was never the same."

"It's confusing."

"Very."

"There are times when I want to scream."

"As loud as you can, yes."

Evelyn turned. "What do I do, Ma? What do I do?"

Winona smiled and hugged her. "You do what every woman before you has done."

"What is that?"

"You follow your heart and hope for the best."

Chapter Ten

The basket held a lot. Evelyn packed a bundle of pemmican at the bottom. She'd helped her mother make it a month ago. Sometimes they made it from buffalo meat, but this time it had been the meat of a buck her father shot. They had cut the meat into strips and dried and salted it, then pounded the strips until the meat was ground fine. Then they added fat and chokecherries. It would last years, and was as tasty as anything.

She went into the pantry and got carrots and wild onions. She cut six slices from a loaf of bread and wrapped the slices in a cloth. She put butter in the basket along with a knife to spread it. She put in a couple of corn cakes left over from a few days ago. Her pa had bought a tin of raisins at Bent's Fort and she took that. She also packed tea. Since they might shoot game for fresh meat, she placed a small pot on top and next to it a spider, a three-legged pan made for cooking over fires.

The sun had not yet risen when Evelyn went out to the corral. She opened the gate and went in and spoke quietly to the horses. Her buttermilk was at the back. She slid on a bridle and brought Buttercup out and put on the saddle blanket. She threw her saddle up and over and cinched it. Then she brought Buttercup around to the front of the cabin and looped the reins around a peg on the wall.

Evelyn walked to the south corner and gazed to the east. There was no sign of Dega yet, but he would be there. He had said he would and he never let her down.

The wind was still, the lake as smooth as glass. In the dark it was like a great black eye staring up at the star-speckled sky. She heard a fish splash and the far-off cry of a loon.

She went inside and sat at the table. For some reason she was nervous. Maybe it was the lying, she told herself. Maybe it was the fact that she would have Dega to herself, exactly as she wanted. Maybe she was nervous because she was afraid of what they might do. She coughed and drummed her fingers and was glad her mother and father were still in bed.

Her eyelids grew heavy and her head drooped. She had hardly slept, she was so excited. She imagined how wonderful it would be, just the two of them. She imagined him kissing her, and tingled.

With a start, Evelyn jerked her head up. She had fallen asleep. A rosy tinge lit the window. She went out and around the cabin. A golden crown lit the eastern horizon. The sun was coming up. She rose onto her toes and stared hard and eagerly, but the shore was empty of life. Oh well, she thought. She had asked him to come as early as he could. Maybe he couldn't get away yet. Maybe his folks had him doing chores. She shrugged and went to the lake and put her hands on her hips, and gave another small start. She was unarmed. She had left her pistols and her rifle inside. If her pa saw her, he would be upset. One of his cardinal rules was that she was never to step outside the cabin without a weapon. Even if it was to feed the chickens or get firewood. She thought it a silly rule, but she didn't care to wash the dishes for a month if she broke it.

Evelyn regretted deceiving them. They had always been honest and forthright with her. And here she was, planning to spend a night alone with a man. The clomp of hooves caused her heart to flutter. She turned, and it seemed to her that although the sun was not fully up, the rider approaching was awash in light and she could see every detail as clearly as at midday. He wore green buckskins, as always. Over his back was a quiver and a bow. He had brought a lance, too, a gift to him from Shakespeare, who had lived with various Indian tribes and could fashion a weapon as well as any of them. She went along the shore a short way and stopped to await him.

"Dega," she said softly to herself.

Degamawaku saw Evelyn King come past the cabin and inwardly winced. He was happy that they were to spend the day together, and yet he was deeply troubled. His mother's words were a great weight on his shoulders. He had tossed and turned all night, unable to get them out of his head. He drew rein and smiled down at the loveliest face he had ever seen. "Good morning, Evelyn." He had practiced that "good morning" until he could say it exactly as she did.

"Good morning, handsome."

Dega knew that word well. She called him handsome a lot. It meant he was pleasing to her eyes. "How you be?" he asked, and caught himself. "Sorry. How are you?"

"I am fine now." Evelyn yearned to reach up and

pull him down and kiss him, but she contained herself. "I'm looking forward to this day so much."

"I, too," Dega said. He had learned to keep his responses simple. His English was nowhere as near as good as he would like it to be. The less he spoke, the less apparent it was.

"I'll be right back." Evelyn hurried inside. She had left her pistols and the Hawken on the table; she wedged the flintlocks under her belt and cradled the rifle in the crook of her elbow, then went to the counter for the basket. When she turned, her mother was in the doorway to the bedroom pulling her robe about her. "Ma. You're up."

"I am always up at dawn," Winona said. "Your father is getting dressed."

Evelyn hefted the basket. "Tell him I love him." She was almost to the front door when her mother said her name. "Yes?"

"You gave your word to him."

"About what?" Evelyn asked, knowing full well.

"That Dega and you will be home by dark. We are holding you to it. Do not disappoint us."

Evelyn hoped she wasn't blushing from the shame she felt. "Haven't I always done as you've asked?"

"Almost always," Winona said.

Evelyn smiled and nodded. "Don't worry. Dega won't let anything happen to me."

"It is what you might do to yourself that concerns me more."

"What do you mean?"

"You know very well."

"See you tonight, Ma," Evelyn said, and got out of there. She couldn't bear to look her mother in the eye. Quickly, she tied the basket to her saddle, mounted, and reined the buttermilk next to Dega's sorrel. "I'll lead the way."

"I will follow," Dega said. It occurred to him that when they went on rides together, she nearly always led. He had never given it much thought, but now that he did, it bothered him.

Evelyn clucked to Buttercup and poked with her heels. She passed the corral and was midway to the forest when she glanced back. Her mother and father had come out of the cabin. Her father raised his arm and waved. She returned the favor and said under her breath, "I'm sorry, Pa."

The woods closed around them. Here and there were oaks and a few mahoganies, but the forest was principally evergreens: ponderosa pine, lodgepole pine, and Douglas fir. Higher up were aspens and spruce.

The air had a pine scent that Evelyn always liked. Wildlife was everywhere. Ground squirrels scampered about. Tree squirrels leaped from limb to limb. Rabbits bounded away in fright and marmots whistled from atop their burrows. Once a porcupine waddled away, bristling with quills. Evelyn lost count of the number of deer she saw. Most were does. The older bucks were too wary to be abroad during the day; it was the younger ones, the spikes, that braved the sun.

The woods were a bird paradise. Sparrows chirped and crossbills beeped. Siskins made a peculiar buzzing sound. Jays screeched and woodpeckers *rat-a-tat-tatted*. Vultures circled lazily in search of carrion, and hawks circled in search of prey. Eagles were the masters of the sky.

Ordinarily Evelyn drank in the scenery and the

pulsing throb of life with relish, but today her enthusiasm was directed at the rider behind her. She couldn't stop looking back at him. It got so, she willed herself to face front so he wouldn't think she was being silly.

Dega wondered why she kept glancing back. Once or twice he could understand, but twenty or thirty times made him wonder if she was afraid he would change his mind and turn around. She needn't have worried. He needed to have a talk with her. He needed to know if his mother was right.

Evelyn found the pass without difficulty. It was at the base of a rock cliff, a narrow gap invisible from below. Deer and elk tracks were proof it saw regular use. The far end opened onto a timbered valley. She reined to the north, toward a serrated ridge fringed by firs.

Dega was surprised. He'd thought they were coming to the valley they had visited before. "Where we go?" he called up to her.

"You'll see," Evelyn answered. Once the sun went down and she didn't show up, her father would come after her. Maybe her mother, too. They might think to take the pass into the valley below, but they would never expect her to cross over into the next valley to the north. Even if they did suspect, tracking at night was hard and slow, even if they used torches. At the very least it would take them another day to find her. Which suited her just fine.

It was the middle of the afternoon when they crossed over. Evelyn drew rein on a grassy shelf and pointed. "Look there. Is that a perfect place for a picnic or what?'

Below lay a small valley split by a narrow stream.

The valley floor was lush with high grass, the slopes dense with trees.

"We need perfect place?" Dega asked. As near as he could remember, "perfect" meant the best that something could be. *Any* place was fine by him.

"I want it to be a day we'll remember for as long as we live," Evelyn told him.

"Picnic important?"

"Everything we do is important to me."

The ride down took half an hour. Evelyn had seldom seen forest so thick. At times they had to force their way through. At length they came out of the shadows and into the high grass. Only then did it hit her how quiet it was. "Listen. You can almost hear your heartbeat."

Dega raised his head but heard nothing. Certainly not his heart. The stillness was unusual. Only a few times in the past had he ever known it to be so quiet.

Evelyn reined toward the stream. She was tired and her throat was dry. On a low bank she drew rein. Sliding down, she arched her spine and pressed her hand to the small of her back. "All that riding about put a kink in me."

Dega tried to decipher her comment. A kink, to the best of his recollection, was a bend or twist, like the time Nate King had a kink in a rope and had to unravel it. He did not see a kink in Evelyn. "I am glad it not put one," he said for a loss of anything better. Alighting, he went down the bank, dropped onto a knee, set his lance on the ground, and dipped his hand in the water. It was runoff from on high, and cold. He splashed some on his neck and face, then cupped his palm and sipped.

Evelyn quenched her own thirst. She had set the

Hawken down to use both hands, and admired Dega over her fingers. When she was done she wiped her hands on her dress and said, "Well."

Dega wondered if he was supposed to say anything to that. He tried a "Well," of his own.

"Here we are."

Where else would they be? Dega asked himself. All he said was "Yes."

Evelyn stood and turned in a slow circle. "It's pretty here, don't you think?"

"It quiet."

"That will change once the wind picks up and the sun starts to go down," Evelyn predicted. By then the meat-eaters would be stirring and fill the night with their howls and roars and screams.

"We have picnic here?" Dega asked, and patted the ground.

"We could so the water is handy," Evelyn said. But the truth was, a secluded nook was more to her fancy. She pointed at the woods to the west. "I'd like over yonder better."

"What you wish," Dega said. Until that moment he hadn't realized how they nearly always did what she wanted and rarely what he wanted. The same as how she led when they went riding.

Evelyn's saddle creaked as she swung up. "Let's go, Buttercup," she said, and flicked the reins.

Dega trailed after her. Conflicting tides of emotion were tearing at him. He had much he wanted to say once they made camp, but he was afraid to say it for fear he would lose her.

Evelyn hummed as she rode. She couldn't wait to set up camp. She imagined how it would be that evening around the fire, talking, and other things, and she grew warm in anticipation. Then Buttercup snorted and stopped, and she looked up. "Oh my."

Dega drew rein beside her. He saw what she was looking at. "Someone live here."

"Surely not," Evelyn said. Yet there was the evidence, right in front of her eyes: a lodge made of limbs and brush with a hide over the entrance. By Shoshone standards it was crude. A vague memory tugged at her, and she said, "I know who made that."

"You do?"

"Sheepeaters."

"Sorry?" Dega had heard mention of many new tribes since his family came to the mountains but never a tribe by that name.

"The Tukaduka. My pa says they're related to the Shoshones, but they don't live like the Shoshones do." Evelyn gigged her horse closer. Suddenly a foul odor assailed her, and she almost gagged.

"Look!" Dega exclaimed.

Evelyn stopped in alarm. The body of a woman lay near the hide, which she now saw was ripped and torn as if by razor-sharp knives. Jerking her Hawken up, she probed the woods beyond. "We better have a look-see."

Dega firmed his grip on his lance. He'd never expected to find death in so remote a place, yet if there was one thing he had learned about the wilderness, it was to expect the unexpected. "This bad, yes?"

"This is very bad," Evelyn King said.

Chapter Eleven

The dark one stirred in his lair and sat up. He was uneasy and his shoulder was bothering him. Rising, he padded onto the ledge and gazed over his domain. He listened and sniffed the air. Birds warbled in the trees. Other than that, the valley he had claimed was quiet and peaceful.

He paced back and forth. It was early, and he didn't yet feel the pangs of hunger that nightly impelled him to prowl in search of prey. A pair of ravens flapped overhead and he watched them fly off.

The dark one went into the niche in the rock cliff and lay on his belly with his chin on his forepaws. He closed his eyes and dozed. Images filled his head, and his legs twitched. He was running after a doe. He could see the white of her tail and her pumping legs, and he leaped and landed on her back. He bit her neck and slashed with his claws and she crashed down, thrashing and pumping her rich wet blood over him and the grass. He growled and lapped it, and then he was awake again and raised his head.

His uneasiness persisted. He went back out to the ledge. The sun was warm on his body. Lethargy crept over him, and he dozed again. When next he woke, the gray shadows of twilight were spreading and the hunger was on him.

Descending, the dark one tested the wind. Elk had passed by recently. Usually they were higher up, but they had come to graze on the succulent grass. His nose to the ground, he set out on their trail. There were two, a cow and her calf. He walked faster. Calf meat was juicy and sweet.

Their scent hung heavy around a thicket. They were still in there. His keen ears detected the rustling of their bodies. They had lain up in its depths for the day and would soon emerge to feed. They didn't know he was there; he never let his presence be known.

Circling, the dark one came to a small pine and sank flat under it. The low branches hid him. With the eternal patience of his kind, he waited for his quarry to show.

The sun had been swallowed by the western peaks when the thicket crackled. The mother came out first, raised her head to sniff, and pricked her ears. She was cautious, as all good mothers were, but the dark one wasn't upwind and she didn't smell him. She snorted, the signal for her calf to emerge. A male born that spring, it wasn't half her size.

The dark one focused on the calf. The mother would be harder to kill and he always went for the easiest. There was less chance of being hurt and he could not afford another injury. His limp was a constant reminder of how costly a mistake could be.

The pair started down, the mother in the lead. She was wary and stopped every few steps to look about. She sensed something was amiss, but she didn't know what.

The dark one tensed his muscles. The calf was

looking at her, cuing his action on hers. That was usually the way with the young. It made them vulnerable. It made them slow to react. He bared his fangs but made no sound. Not yet. Not until the kill.

The mother twisted her neck to look behind them. She stared right at the small pine and then looked away. She hadn't seen him. His dark coat and the dark shadows were one.

The calf stamped as if impatient.

The dark one was ready. When the mother turned, he exploded from under the pine. Two bounds and he was on them. He leaped high and landed on the calf's back, his weight almost smashing it to the ground. It bleated and tried to run, but its legs were wobbly. The dark one sank his teeth deep into its throat even as his claws churned and sliced. The mother bleated, too, and tried to butt him. He wrenched with his fangs, and a red geyser sprayed his face. The calf took several staggering steps and collapsed. The dark one clung on, tearing and raking. A pain in his side caused him to yowl in fury. The mother had butted him. She drew back and lowered her head to charge again. A black blur, he whirled to confront her. He snarled and spat, his tail lashing. She hesitated. She bleated again, and sniffed, and drew back. Her calf had stopped moving. Whirling, she plowed off into the gathering night.

The dark one let her go. He had what he wanted. He sank onto the calf, lapped at its ravaged throat, and purred. Here was life's most delicious treat. He loved to lap blood. Meat was good but blood was best. When there was no more blood to be had, he tore off a great chunk of raw flesh and chewed. Around him the world darkened. Stars glimmered. In the woods an owl hooted. Far off a coyote wailed. Farther away, a wolf howled. The other meat-eaters were abroad.

The dark one gorged. When his belly was full, he rose and turned his back to the calf and scratched grass and dirt onto it. He would come back to eat several times.

Cool night air washed over his sinewy form as he loped up the mountain. He caught the scent of a black bear. He had come across it twice already, a big male in its prime. Were it a male of his own kind, he would challenge it for the valley. But bears were not competitors for the same meat; they seldom went after deer or elk. So long as this bear left him alone, he would leave it alone.

He was almost to the ledge when the wind shifted. A new scent caused him to stop in his tracks. He raised his head to pinpoint where the scent was coming from, but the wind shifted. A growl escaped him. It was the scent he hated. The scent he was reminded of every time he put weight on what was left of his forepaw.

Irritated, the dark one climbed to his lair. He stretched out on the ledge and closed his eyes, but sleep eluded him. He was strangely restless. He rose to go into the niche, and froze.

Down on the valley floor a light glimmered. He has seen lights like it before. He had seen the flames that made it and those who made the flames, the two-legged creatures he hated, the creatures responsible for crippling him.

The creatures he would slay.

Evelyn King breathed shallow as she stepped to the body. The stink was atrocious. Using the stock of her

Hawken, she rolled the body over. A beetle scuttled from an eye socket, and she recoiled.

"Poor woman," Dega said. Whites said that a lot when bad things happened to others. Which perplexed him. He understood the whites' ideas of "poor" and "rich" but not how having a bad thing happen made someone "poor."

Although she didn't want to, Evelyn bent down. The body had been there awhile. Scavengers had been at it. Most of the flesh was gone. Only a few shreds of skin remained. Punctures high on the brow gave a clue to the manner of death. "An animal did this."

Dega gazed about them. The grass had been trampled and worn, and in a patch of dirt was a large print. He squatted and pointed. "Cat," he said. "Much big cat." Catching himself, he amended, "Sorry. Very big cat."

Evelyn came over. "A mountain lion." It was rare for painters to attack people. Her father, in all his years in the Rockies, had only ever been attacked by mountain lions twice, so far as she knew. Bears, on the other hand, he'd clashed with often.

"How long you think she be dead?" Dega asked.

Evelyn shrugged. "I'm no judge. Pa and my brother would likely know just by looking at her. If I had to guess, I'd say a week, two at the most." She turned to the lodge. "Anyone in there?" she called out. When there was no answer she switched to Shoshone. "*Ne hainji.*" No one replied. She pushed on the hide, and her stomach churned. The stench was worse. Ducking, she warily entered. "Oh my."

Another body was inside. The scavengers had not been at it, but it had rotted and the maggots had done their grisly work. Evelyn gave it a quick scrutiny. "This one was a boy," she reckoned. Not much younger than Dega, she reckoned.

"Cat again?"

"Yes," Evelyn said. Slash marks on the dead boy's buckskins confirmed it. "Let's get out of here." She pushed on the hide and took Buttercup's reins and walked toward the stream. The stink faded and she could breathe again. She sucked air into her lungs and declared, "Thank God."

Dega shared her revulsion. He never liked being around dead things. The Nansusequa always buried their dead within a day of death, usually with a feast and singing to celebrate passing to the other side. They didn't weep and cut themselves as some tribes did. To them, death was a cause for happiness, not sorrow. "Those mother and son, you think?"

"Maybe," Evelyn said. It begged the question of what had happened to the father. Could be the painter had gotten him, too.

"We bury them?"

Evelyn debated. That was the proper thing, she supposed. But there wasn't much left of either the woman or the boy. And it wasn't as if they were kin or even Shoshones. They were strangers. She felt no obligation. Besides, it would take time she would rather spend more pleasantly. "I think we should leave them where they are for their own people to find."

"If you say," Dega said. Though in his opinion a person should show respect for the dead as well as the living.

"We'll go up the valley a ways and make camp," Evelyn proposed. She mounted and clucked to

Buttercup. She tried to shut the bodies from her mind and think only of Dega. "Are you hungry?"

"Not after them."

Neither was Evelyn. The grisly find had spoiled her mood and her appetite. She refused to be discouraged, though. She had gone to all this trouble to be alone with him, and by God, she wasn't going to let anything spoil it. Forcing a smile, she said, "We can't let all the food I brought go to waste."

Dega was shocked. That she could think of eating amazed him. "We eat later if that all right."

For over a quarter of a mile Evelyn stuck to the tree line. She came on a spot where a crescent of grass indented the forest, and said merrily, "Look what we have here. This will do just fine."

"What about cat?" Dega asked.

"It's long gone by now," Evelyn assured him. "My pa says they roam a large area. Fifty to a hundred miles or better." She was more worried about a grizzly happening by. "We're safe enough."

"I hope," Dega said.

Evelyn untied the picnic basket. From her parfleche she took a short stake, and using a rock, pounded the stake into the ground. She tied one end of a length of rope to the stake and looped the other end over Buttercup's neck. "So she won't stray," she said when she noticed Dega looking at her.

"What I do with my horse?"

"I have more rope. We'll tie off yours, too."

Next Evelyn stripped off her saddle and saddle blanket. She was lowering the saddle when she realized Dega was still standing there. "Something the matter?"

"No." Dega had been on the verge of bringing up

the issue his mother had raised, but he couldn't muster the courage.

"Make yourself useful. Fetch some firewood."

"I be right back." Dega went into the woods. The shadows were lengthening and it was uncommonly still. He marveled at the absence of life. In King Valley there were animals everywhere, but here all he saw were a few birds. His search for fallen limbs took him an arrow's flight from the clearing. He was bending to pick up a short branch when an impression in the bare earth caught his attention: another cat print, only this one was smaller. To him it appeared as if part of the paw was missing.

Dega straightened. He hoped Evelyn was right about the mountain lion being gone. They were fierce fighters, those big cats. Troubled by his find, he started back. Without warning, the undergrowth to his left rustled. He turned and spied a vague shape low to the ground. Dropping the firewood, he raised his lance. He glimpsed what he took for a tawny hide and tensed, but whatever it was, it ran. He took several steps to try to get a better look, but the thing was gone. He waited to be sure it didn't circle around. When he was convinced it was safe, he picked up the firewood and struck off for the clearing, more troubled than ever.

Evelyn was waiting for him. She had spread a blanket and set the food out. "There you are. I was beginning to think you got lost."

Dega was insulted. His people prided themselves on their woodcraft. He could tell direction by the sun and the stars and had never been lost in his entire life. But he didn't mention that. Instead he said, "I see something."

"What?"

"I not know."

"Was it the mountain lion?"

"I think too small," Dega said.

"Good. That's the last thing we need." Evelyn patted the ground. "Why don't you set that wood down and we'll get the fire going?" She opened her parfleche and took out a fire steel and flint and her small box of tinder. Her father had taught her how to light a fire when she was little and she was so adept at it that in no time she had puffed a tiny flame to life and their fire was crackling and growing. She put the steel and flint and box in her parfleche and turned to Dega, who had sat across from her. "You can sit closer if you want. That way I don't have to reach across to hand you food."

Dega had never really noticed how she was always telling him what to do. He slid around the fire and she handed him a piece of pemmican.

"Help yourself to whatever else you want." Evelyn was tickled. Here they were, at long last. She gazed on his handsome features and felt a stirring deep inside.

Normally Dega would be famished, but he was nervous, which wasn't normal for him at all. "We need talk."

"Yes," Evelyn agreed. "We do."

Just then a twig snapped and they both glanced at the ring of woods.

Something was staring back at them.

Chapter Twelve

For a few anxious moments Evelyn thought it was the mountain lion. Then she realized that the eye shine was different; the eyes were round, not slanted. "What is that?" she whispered.

Dega didn't know. He went to rise and suddenly the thing spun, scrambling on all fours, just as it had done when he saw it before. His lance in hand, he ran to the woods.

Evelyn was quick to catch up. She raised the Hawken to her shoulder, but whatever it had been was gone. "This valley is starting to spook me."

"Maybe we should go," Dega said, proud that he got the English right.

"No." Evelyn refused to be deprived of their night together. She had gone to great lengths. She had even lied to her parents. "It was probably just a rabbit."

"Big for rabbit," Dega said.

"Well, it sure wasn't the cat that killed those poor Sheepeaters." Evelyn lowered the Hawken and made bold to take his hand. "Come on. Let's finish our meal."

There was so much Evelyn wanted to say, and now that she had the opportunity, she couldn't bring herself to. She spread butter on a slice of bread and took a bite and chewed but didn't taste it.

Dega nibbled a piece of pemmican. He had held

off as long as he could. Then, taking a deep breath, he asked, "You like me, yes?"

"I more than like you," Evelyn responded. Here was her chance to come right out and say what was in her heart, but her tongue stuck to the roof of her mouth.

"I more than like you," Dega said. "I more than like you very much."

"You don't know how happy you've just made me."

"Happy is good." Dega struggled to say it right. So many English words had different meanings or shades of meaning that choosing the best was difficult. "Want to ask question."

"Ask away." Evelyn smiled to encourage him.

"Could be we go on liking more than much?" Dega had to force his mouth to say the next part. "Could be we want be husband and wife?"

Evelyn's heart gave a flutter. "Yes?" she said breathlessly.

"What then?" Dega asked.

"Sorry?" Evelyn said, mildly confused. "How do you mean?"

"What we do after?"

"I reckon we'd do as most married folks do," Evelyn replied. "Live together. Do things together." The idea of one of those things made her cheeks grow warm.

"Have little ones?"

Evelyn grew warmer and coughed. "Having babies is part of married life. Why? Are you hankering to have some?" She thought her ears were about to burn off.

"I like maybe have son one day," Dega said. "Teach him as Father teach me. It be great funness."

Evelyn didn't correct him. "And you want to know how I feel about having kids, is that it?"

"No," Dega said. "I want know about . . ." He stopped and racked his brain. "About how you want teach them."

"Teach them what?" Evelyn asked, confused again.

"Teach them all there be."

Evelyn had a ready answer. "I would teach them as my mother and father taught me. How to live, how to do things. More important, I would teach them to be honest and true." She felt a twinge of conscience at that.

"You teach white ways?" Dega voiced his innermost concern.

"White ways. Shoshone ways. All that I have learned I would pass on to them."

"Oh."

Evelyn was puzzled by the disappointment in his voice. "Isn't that what any parent would do?"

"What about Nansusequa ways?"

"We would teach them those, too. It goes without saying," Evelyn assured him.

"Nansusequa and white and Shoshone," Dega said.

"Yes."

"All three."

"Doesn't that make sense?"

Until his talk with his mother, Dega would have agreed it made perfect sense. Now he harbored doubts. "Then they not be Nansusequa."

"What are you talking about? If you teach your children your ways, they will be as Nansusequa as you are."

"No. They be white and Shoshone, too. Only be Nansusequa if they only learn Nansusequa."

Evelyn was trying to comprehend his insistence
"I was raised white and Shoshone, and look at me."

"You mostly white."

"Not entirely," Evelyn objected, even though he
was right. She'd never taken to the Shoshone way of
life as fully as her brother. Not that she had any
thing against them. She had just always favored her
father's side of the family, not just in looks. She liked
to eat white food and to wear white clothes and she
had loved town and city life. How strange, then, that
she was in love with someone who wasn't white.

"I need children be Nansusequa," Dega said
"Only Nansusequa. Not white. Not Shoshone."

"Oh," Evelyn said, deeply disturbed. "When did
you come to that conclusion?" This was the first she
had heard of it.

As they talked, the valley darkened with the on
set of night. In the distance carnivores made their
presence known.

"The day before this one. What it be called again?"

"Yesterday."

"Yes. Yesterday," Dega said, bobbing his chin.

"What brought it on? Why is it suddenly so impor
tant to you that your children be raised Nansusequa
and only Nansusequa?"

Dega helped himself to a carrot and bit off the end
He chewed slowly, the crunch loud in his ears. "Im
portant not just me. Important for people."

"But you five are the last Nansusequas left," Eve
lyn brought up. "You *are* your people."

"Want more of us," Dega explained. "Want many
Nansusequa. Like before white men attacked vil
lage."

"You aim to rebuild your tribe?" Evelyn was ap

alled that he was bringing this up now, of all times. She reached over and placed her hand on his. "We can talk more about this when we get back."

"Now," Dega said.

"Why is it so blamed important?" Evelyn was growing annoyed. All the trouble she had gone to, and he threw this into her lap. "You and me wouldn't have kids for a good many years."

"Must find out now."

"Why, consarn it?"

"So have right woman."

His reply was akin to a physical blow to Evelyn's gut. He was saying she might not be right for him. "Let me be sure I savvy. You're saying that any children of yours have to be raised as Nansusequa and nothing but Nansusequa?"

"Yes," Dega confirmed, happy that he had gotten his point across.

"And you don't give a hoot about the wife's feelings? She can go to Hades for all you care?"

Dega was worried; she sounded mad. He remembered that "hoot" was the sound an owl made. How that applied in this instance was a mystery. So was "Hades." Shakespeare McNair had used that word once or twice and he recalled it had something to do with people who lived deep underground. So if he understood Evelyn, she was saying he was not sounding like an owl and he wanted his wife to live under the earth.

"You're not being reasonable," Evelyn said. "If a person is half-and-half and she has a baby, there is nothing wrong with her wanting to raise it whichever half she'd like."

"You want raise baby white and Nansusequa?"

"That's fairest."

Dega was torn between his mother's appeal and Evelyn's logic. Both had merit. But his mother had touched him deeply with her desire to see their tribe reborn. The Nansusequa could rise again—only if he and his sisters stood firm in how their children were to be reared. Suddenly standing, he declared, "I must think." The hurt that came into Evelyn's eyes made his gut tighten. She was upset and he couldn't blame her. Wheeling, he crossed to the forest. Clenching his fists in anger at how their outing had been spoiled, he realized he had left his lance by the fire.

Evelyn was in despair. Always before, they talked their differences out. Granted, most were minor and she had come to think that they saw eye to eye on most everything. This new spat didn't bode well for their future. She reached for the tin of raisins and put it down again. She wasn't hungry anymore.

Dega stopped and looked back. He wanted to go to Evelyn and embrace her and tell her everything would be fine, provided she agreed to bring up their children as Nansusequa. He took a step, and froze. A stealthy scrape had come out of the undergrowth to his left. Fingers flying, he unslung his bow and set the string. He slid an arrow from his quiver and nocked the shaft and drew the string, the barbed tip trained on the vegetation. It could be a deer. It could be a rabbit. It could be the beast that slew the Sheepeaters.

Something moved.

Dega strained his eyes. The thing appeared to be on all fours. He stood his ground, aware that if he loosed his shaft it might be deflected by intervening brush. Let the creature come closer, he told himself. Let it come out where he couldn't miss. It was staring at him, as if curious. His fingers began to hurt from the strain of keeping the string pulled.

Suddenly the thing started toward him.

Over by the fire, Evelyn decided to try to hash out their differences. She gripped her Hawken and entered the woods, where she saw he had an arrow to his bow. "Dega?" she asked in concern. "What is it?"

Dega saw the shape stop and turn toward her. He still hadn't had a good look at it.

"Dega? Didn't you hear me?"

Like a rush of wind, the thing was off. Dega glimpsed pumping limbs—and something else. He blinked in surprise, and the apparition was no longer there. Lowering his bow, he plunged into the brush after it, certain he must be mistaken. Ahead, the shape flitted between two trees. He ran faster, but when he got to the same trees, beyond was a wall of woodland awash in the pale glow of the full moon, and nothing else. "Where did you get to?" he asked out loud in his own tongue.

"What did you see?" Evelyn came to his side, breathing heavily from their sprint.

"I saw . . . thing," Dega said.

"Was it the mountain lion?"

"No."

"Then what?"

Dega shrugged, a typically white gesture he had learned from her. "It ran off."

Evelyn lowered her Hawken. "Well, if it wasn't a lion and it wasn't a bear, we have nothing to worry about."

Dega was inclined to agree, but ferocity came in

small sizes as well as big. Wolverines weren't half as large as bears, yet they were every bit as formidable.

"Want to head back?"

"Wait." Dega hoped for another glimpse. It had to have been a trick of the light, but he needed to be sure. The woods stayed silent save for the sigh of the wind and the keening of a fox.

Evelyn shifted her weight from one foot to the other. They were wasting time, in her estimation. "I'd really like to talk more about this Nansusequa business."

"Children must be Nansusequa," Dega declared. Or it would crush his mother and be the end of his people, forever.

"Dang it," Evelyn said. "Why are you being so pigheaded?"

This was a new one to Dega. A pig was an animal the whites raised. He had seen a few and their heads were nothing like his. "I do what must," he said. Since the thing in the woods was gone, he wheeled and made for the fire. He sat cross-legged with the bow across his legs and glumly stared into the flames.

Evelyn had never seen him behave this way. She walked around and sat on the other side, her rifle in her lap. On the heights to the west a bear roared. To the northeast a wolf raised an ululating cry to the moon. She barely noticed. Neither was near enough to pose a danger. "I thought you cared for me."

"I do," Dega said.

"Then what in the world is going on? Why are you acting this way? You never said anything about this Nansusequa stuff before."

"Not think of it before."

"What brought it on?"

Dega hesitated. She might become mad at his mother if he told her the truth, so he said, "It bring on itself."

Evelyn lapsed into silence. She supposed that from his point of view it was fitting that his children be raised Nansusequa. But to *only* raise them Nansusequa was asking too much. Besides, how could she, when she wasn't a Nansusequa herself? She had no objection to learning their ways, but she couldn't just stop being part white and part Shoshone. It was ingrained into her. She put her elbows on her knees and her chin in her hands and stared sadly at the picnic basket. Her getaway had been ruined.

Dega had never seen her so sorrowful. He squirmed and bowed his head and wondered if he was asking too much of her. Which led him to wondering if his mother was asking too much of him. He and his sisters were the last of their kind, yes. Unless he married one of them—and the Nansusequa never did that—any woman he took for his wife would have beliefs and habits of her own and would desire to raise their children accordingly. How, then, could he raise his children strictly as Nansusequa? He ran a hand over his brow. All this thinking was hurting his head.

Evelyn happened to gaze past him and stiffened. Something had appeared at the edge of the clearing. Not the mountain lion, something else. She discerned a low hump that could be . . . anything . . . watching them. "We have company," she quietly announced.

Dega snapped out of himself. "Where?"

"Behind you. Don't turn around. We don't want

to spook it." Evelyn put another branch on the fire and the flames grew. So did the circle of firelight but not far enough to reach the . . . thing.

"Maybe it what we chase."

"Do you have any notion what it is?"

Dega did, but his eyes might have been mistaken. "Night play trick on me. I not sure."

"It's not big enough to be a threat," Evelyn said. "Maybe it will just go away." The next moment, to her astonishment, the thing started to grow. It rose until it was three times as tall. Its silhouette was too vague for her to identify, but one fact was apparent. "My God! It's standing on two legs."

Not only that, it was coming toward them.

Chapter Thirteen

Evelyn held her breath. She wrapped her hands around the Hawken, ready to jerk it up and shoot.

Dega looked over his shoulder. He had been right, then. The night hadn't played tricks on him. "It is a person."

Evelyn had reached the same conclusion. She forced a smile and said, "How do you do?"

Whoever it was halted just beyond the firelight.

"Do you speak English?" Evelyn asked, and when she got no response, she asked the same thing in Shoshone.

The figure stood motionless.

"We're friendly," Evelyn said. "We're only staying the night." She noticed that the horses had raised their heads and were staring at the figure. Neither betrayed any alarm. "Why don't you come closer? We won't hurt you."

The figure stayed where it was.

"What do we do?" Evelyn whispered to Dega.

"We not move," Dega said. It pleased him that she had asked his opinion instead of telling him what to do.

Evelyn had a thought. She picked up a corn cake and held it out. "Would you like something to eat? There's plenty if you're hungry and we're more than happy to share."

The figure took a step and the firelight played over it.

Astonishment caused Evelyn to stiffen and blurt, "My God! It's a little girl!"

The child was dirty and disheveled, her face smeared with grime. Her buckskin dress was filthy and torn. Her knees had been scraped raw. Her eyes were pools of fear.

Evelyn went to rise and stopped. The instant she moved, the girl took a step back. "Wait," she urged, and willed herself to keep her voice calm. "Don't go. You're welcome here."

"We are not your enemies, child," Dega said in Nansusequa. "I bid you welcome in peace."

The girl raised a hand to her matted hair and scratched.

"Why won't she speak?" Evelyn wondered. "Who can she be, wandering around in the dark all alone?" In a flash of inspiration, the explanation came to her. "I'm so stupid."

"What?"

"That lodge we found. The dead woman and the dead boy." Evelyn nodded at the girl. "She must be part of the same family." Evelyn tried to communicate anew with *"Behne."*

The girl didn't answer.

"Pehnaho."

Still no response.

Evelyn tried, *"Ne dei'."* It was Shoshone for, *I am a friend.* But it brought no reply, either. To Dega she said, "How can we get her to talk?"

"I not know."

"Ne qai neetsiiqwa en." Evelyn had told the girl that she wouldn't hurt her. Once again, with no result.

"Keep trying," Dega urged.

"Kui yekwi."

"What that one?"

"I asked her to come sit with us," Evelyn translated. She moved her hand that held the corn cake to her lap and saw the girl follow the movement. Another inspiration struck. *"Deka,"* she said, and tossed the cake.

It landed a foot or so from the girl. She took a step and reached for it but then cast an anxious glance at them and drew her arm back.

"It is yours," Evelyn said in Shoshone. "Eat it." She couldn't remember if the Tukaduka spoke the exact same dialect as her mother's people, but the tongues were close enough that the girl should be able to understand her. "Damn, I wish she would say something," she whispered to Dega, and then realized what she had said. "Don't tell my pa I cussed or he'll want to wash out my mouth with soap."

"What is cussed?" Dega couldn't recall hearing the word before.

"I said 'damn' and ladies aren't supposed to swear."

"What is swear?"

"It's when you use bad words."

Once again, Dega was confused. "How words be bad?"

"You know. Words that people say when they're mad. Or words about things people shouldn't talk about."

Dega sighed in frustration. He had absolutely no idea what she was talking about. The Nansusequa used the same words whether they were mad or not. "Why ladies not say those words?"

"Don't ask me. It's all right for men to use them

but not women, although when I was back in the States I heard plenty of women swear worse than my pa ever does." Evelyn had forgotten the girl. She looked over and smiled.

The girl had picked up the corn cake and was tearing ravenously at it with her teeth. She made mewing sounds as she ate, as if the food were delicious beyond compare.

"Look at her."

"I see," Dega said.

"The poor thing is starved." Evelyn took another corn cake and threw it. This one landed at the girl's feet. Quick as thought, the girl pounced on it and commenced to gobble both at once, virtually stuffing them into her mouth.

"Where she live?" Dega brought up.

Evelyn had been wondering the same thing. The state the girl was in—filthy and famished—suggested she must be on her own, all alone in the wilderness. That she had lasted this long was a miracle. Smiling, she said in Shoshone, "When you are done eating those cakes, come and sit by the fire with us and we will share more of our food with you."

The girl stopped and stared at her.

"You do understand," Evelyn guessed. She patted the ground. "Sit by me, little one."

Her fright transparent, the girl straightened and took a step. What was left of the two cakes was clutched tight in her hands.

"Neither of us will touch you," Evelyn said. "We want to help."

The girl took another step.

"How are you called?" Evelyn asked. "My name is Blue Flower." It was her Shoshone name, bestowed on her at birth by her mother. "I would like to know yours."

Dega was impressed at how Evelyn was so earnest and nice. The girl was impressed, too, because she came closer and stopped just out of reach. Crumbs speckled her dirty chin. He smiled to show that he, too, was friendly, and said in his own tongue, "We welcome you."

"You must have a name," Evelyn said in Shoshone. "Is it Morning Dove? Little Fawn? Rabbit Tail?" All were names of girls she knew.

The girl went on chewing.

"Is it Buffalo Hump?" Evelyn asked, referring to a noted warrior, and chuckled in amusement. She wasn't sure but she thought the corners of the girl's thin mouth quirked upward. "Is it Bear Running? Drags The Rope? Touch The Clouds?" Again, all names of warriors.

The girl took another bite of corn cake.

"I know." Evelyn grinned. "It must be Cat By The Tail." She meant it to make the girl smile and realized her mistake the moment the words were out of her mouth. The girl recoiled and stopped chewing and cast apprehensive looks over her shoulders.

"It all right," Dega said in English. "No cat here."

The girl turned toward Evelyn. Her eyes shimmered with tears and she tried to speak.

"We will not let anything hurt you," Evelyn assured her. "We are friends." She touched her chest. *"Dei'."* She pointed at Degamawaku. *"Hainji."*

The girl took a step back.

"Wait!" Evelyn reached for her.

Uttering a plaintive wail, the girl whirled and bolted.

"Catch her!" Evelyn cried, and was up and running. She had always been fleet of foot and she ran full out, but the girl was incredibly swift and widened her lead.

Dega sped to help. He had raced Evelyn once and beaten her, but it had taken all he had. Now he ran full out and caught up just as she reached the woods. He plunged in among the pines and oaks, heedless of the limbs that whipped at him and the brush that tore at his legs. He spied the girl and pointed. "There!"

Evelyn hadn't taken her eyes off her. She was determined to catch the child no matter what; a little girl like that shouldn't be left alone in the wild. So far the girl had defied the odds, but no one's luck held forever. Evelyn flew, holding the Hawken at her side so it wouldn't snag.

The girl glanced back, her small feet flying. She still held on to what was left of the corn cakes.

"Don't be afraid!" Evelyn hollered.

"Stop!" Dega shouted.

The girl darted around a small spruce. They were no more than ten feet behind her yet when they rounded the spruce, she had vanished. They stopped in bewilderment.

"Where did she get to?" Evelyn asked, turning right and left. She listened but other than her heavy breathing and Dega's, the forest was quiet.

"I not know," Dega answered. He took a few more steps and cocked his head. "She disappear." He was proud of that word. His English was improving.

"We can't lose her." Evelyn barreled into the dark tangle of vegetation. "Little girl? Where are you?" she yelled in English. Realizing her mistake, she switched to Shoshone.

Dega stayed near Evelyn. Encountering the girl had reminded him of the bodies, a fate he did not care for Evelyn to share.

Evelyn stopped. "She has to be here somewhere." She pointed to the left. "You go that way. I'll go this. Stay in earshot." Without waiting for him to answer, she charged into the darkness.

Dega almost went after her. He didn't consider it a good idea to separate. But she was counting on him to help, so he reluctantly bent his steps in the direction she had indicated. "Little girl?" he called out in Nansusequa and in English.

For a quarter of an hour they roved and hunted until finally Evelyn shouted his name and Dega jogged to meet her. She was sitting on a log, her shoulders slumped in defeat.

"I can't believe she got away from us."

"She like rabbit," Dega said.

"Even so. She's so small." Evelyn thumped the log. "We'll rest a spell and then head back."

"That fine." Dega perched next to her, careful not to let his body brush hers. Just a few days ago he would have rubbed against her on purpose.

"We have to find her. We can't leave until we do."

"Yes," Dega said.

"Can you imagine what she's been through? Her mother and brother killed by that mountain lion and now she's all alone."

"Where be father?"

"Maybe he was killed, too." Evelyn rested the Hawken's butt on the ground and leaned it on the log. "One of us should ride back at first light and fetch my folks."

The suggestion startled Dega. "What?"

"We can use their help. Maybe fetch your folks, too. And the McNairs while you're at it."

"Me?"

"The girl was taking a shine to me. I could tell. She might come if I keep calling. So it has to be me who stays and searches for her while you ride for help."

"No," Dega said flatly.

"Pardon?"

"No," Dega said again. "I not leave you alone."

Evelyn swiveled toward him. "Why on earth not?"

"The cat."

"What about it? It's long gone by now. And I have these." Evelyn patted the Hawken and her flintlocks. "I'll be perfectly fine."

"I not go."

Evelyn's temper flared. Here she was, trying to save that poor girl's life, and he was balking. "I was right about you being pigheaded."

"I not pig."

"You're close enough. Or don't you care that that little girl could die and it would be on your shoulders?"

Here was another mind-twister Dega must unravel. Evelyn seemed to be saying that if the girl died, he must carry her. "Why not dig hole and bury her?"

"What?" Evelyn shook her head. "I must not be making myself plain. That girl won't last much longer by her lonesome. You saw how scrawny she is. She's barely eating enough to stay alive. We have to save her and we have to do it before something happens to her. Do you agree I'm right about all that?"

"Yes," Dega reluctantly conceded.

"Let's say I can lure her in. What then? You and me don't know a lot about raising kids. My mother and my father do. Another reason you have to bring them, and bring them fast."

"But the cat . . ."

"Will you stop harping on that? Have we seen any sign of it? No. I told you they roam a large area. It's probably miles and miles from here." Evelyn put her hand on his arm. "Do you care for me or not?" she asked bluntly.

"I care," Dega said. He cared for her more than he had ever cared for anyone. Which was why he was so torn up inside. His caring for her was at war with his devotion to his mother.

"Then do this for me," Evelyn said. "Fetch my folks. Your folks, too, if you want. Please."

Dega felt all twisted inside. "All right," he heard himself say, although every particle of his being screamed at him that he shouldn't go.

"Good." Evelyn beamed. "We'll get a good night's sleep and you can leave at first light."

"As you want," Dega said.

"Don't look so down at the mouth. You're doing the right thing. Saving that girl is more important than you and me at the moment."

"Evelyn . . ." Dega began. He wanted to tell her about his talk with his mother and why it was important his children be raised as Nansusequas.

"Yes?"

Dega changed his mind. It might make her mad

that his mother objected to raising their children white. "Nothing," he said softly.

"You're sure acting strange tonight." Evelyn had never seen him like this and didn't know what to make of it. She feared that maybe he didn't feel for her as she felt for him.

"Sorry."

"Let's head back and turn in."

The mountains around them were alive with cries. From all quarters came howls and wails and bleats and the occasional roar of a roving grizzly high on the heights. A feline screech revealed the presence of a bobcat.

Not once did Evelyn hear the telltale scream of a painter. She put the food back in the basket and lay on her back on her saddle blanket with her saddle for a pillow. She tossed. She turned. She glanced countless times at the dark woods in the hope the girl would return. She gazed countless times at Dega, too, rolled up in his blanket and not moving, apparently sound asleep.

Dega heard her fidget. He lay with his back to her, unable to sleep except in fits and snatches. His chest felt as if that cat were clawing at it. He yearned to go to her and take her in his arms and tell her that he was sorry and they could raise their children any way she wanted.

But he didn't.

Chapter Fourteen

The rosy blush of dawn painted the eastern sky when Dega climbed on the sorrel. He was stiff and hungry, and he dearly wanted to stay. But Evelyn was still insisting he go, so he looked down at her and said, "You be much careful, Evelyn King."

"Don't worry about me," Evelyn replied. "I've lived in the wilds all my life. I can take care of myself."

Dega lifted the reins, then hesitated. "I not like this."

Evelyn stepped to the rear of his horse. "Off you go, whether you like it or not." She gave the animal a hard smack, then grinned and waved. "Hurry back, you hear!"

"I will!" Dega promised. He wished the little girl would appear so he didn't have to go, but she didn't. He used his heels and brought the sorrel to a trot. The faster he reached King Valley, the better for his peace of mind.

Evelyn watched him ride off with a sinking feeling in her heart. She really didn't want him to leave, but it had to be done. They needed her ma and her pa. Especially her ma. Her mother was good with children. If anyone could persuade that little girl to come in out of the wilds, it was Winona.

Shadowed woodland at the end of the valley swallowed Dega and his mount. Evelyn sighed and went to the fire and hunkered. She had put coffee on. Her pa was powerful fond of it and he had passed that fondness on to her. Now she couldn't start her day without a cup or two.

Her father had tried to instill his love of reading in her, too. He read every evening and often took one of his cherished books to bed with him. She would read when she had nothing better to do. Her brother hardly ever read at all. She'd asked Zach once why he hated to read so much and he said that it made his head hurt. Something about the print on the page didn't agree with him.

The coffee was hot enough. Evelyn filled her tin cup and held it in both hands. She sipped and smacked her lips. She was glad the sun was rising. Ever since she was little, she'd been a smidgen scared of the dark. Her mother said that was natural, but she'd noticed that her brother wasn't scared of it. Her brother wasn't scared of anything.

Evelyn wondered why she was thinking of Zach so much. Maybe it was because of all that talk with Dega about having children, and Zach and his wife were going to have a baby. She opened the picnic basket and helped herself to a piece of pemmican.

The woods were quiet. Almost too quiet. Evelyn probed every shadow for sign of the little Tukaduka. She figured the child must have a hiding place, somewhere she was safe. It could be anywhere.

A golden crown lit creation. The sky rapidly brightened and the valley stirred to life.

Evelyn stayed where she was. She would let the girl come to her rather than go searching. She remembered how hungry the girl had been, and with that in mind she filled a pot with water and added bits of pemmican and carrots and wild onions and let it simmer so that its scent filled the clearing and the breeze would carry the aroma a good long way.

The morning passed as slow as a turtle. Evelyn drank three cups of coffee and couldn't drink any more. The smell of the stew made her mouth water, but she refused to eat.

Now that she was alone, every unusual sound and sight rubbed at her nerves. The rustle of brush, the slightest movement of the vegetation, the distant crash of a limb falling. She kept her Hawken in her lap and a hand on one of her pistols. The truth be known, she didn't like toting the flintlocks everywhere. They were heavy, and after a long walk they were like anchors around her waist. But her pa had instilled in her that one gun was never enough, that one shot didn't always kill.

Evelyn looked down at the Hawken in her lap. Her father had had it custom-made for her by the Hawken brothers in St. Louis. It was shorter and lighter than most Hawkens, but it was powerful enough to drop a buffalo provided she hit the buff in the vitals.

The thing was, Evelyn didn't like to kill. Her brother used to poke fun at her because she wouldn't even shoot rabbits for the supper pot. He had teased her about being too tenderhearted, or as he put it, "weak in the head." Which always made her bristle.

Evelyn never could understand why there was so much killing in the world. Why creatures had to kill other creatures. Why people killed other people. Why people had to kill animals to eat. Her father and mother said that was just the way things were, but that wasn't enough of an answer. She hated to spill blood, human or otherwise. When she was young, that was a large part of the reason she had entertained the notion that she would leave the wilderness one day and live east of the Mississippi, where people could go their whole lives without killing anything except maybe a few flies and mosquitoes.

Evelyn stirred the stew. She raised the wooden spoon to her lips and sipped. Not bad, she thought. The wild onions gave it a potent flavor. She put the spoon in the pot and shifted to relieve a cramp in her leg, and tingled with excitement.

The bait had worked.

Over by an oak stood the little girl. In the daylight she looked worse. Her hair was a tangled mess of dirt with bits of grass and leaves in the tangle. Her dress was a shambles. She was as thin as a broomstick and there were dark shadows under her eyes.

Evelyn almost blurted, My God! Instead she smiled and said quietly in English, "Look who it is." The girl cocked her head and gave her a quizzical look. "Sorry," Evelyn said in Shoshone. "I am happy to see you again. Would you like to sit at my fire?"

The girl didn't move.

"I will not hurt you."

The girl took a couple of wary steps but came no farther.

"You sure are skittish," Evelyn said in English, and once again switched to her mother's tongue. "I am Blue Flower, remember? What is your name? I would very much like to know."

A slight sound escaped the girl's throat.

"I am sorry. I did not hear. Will you say your name again?"

The girl mumbled.

"I still do not understand. You must speak louder."

"Rainbow," the girl said. "Bright Rainbow."

Evelyn chuckled. She had broken through. "That is a pretty name. I like rainbows. Do you like rainbows?"

"Yes."

Evelyn stirred the soup, took a long sip, and smacked her lips. "Are you hungry?"

Bright Rainbow stared longingly at the pot. She rubbed her belly and said, "Very hungry."

Evelyn patted the ground. "Then come eat. I have plenty. And after you have eaten we can talk."

"Where is the man?" Bright Rainbow asked.

"I sent my friend away so he would not scare you. There is just you and me." Evelyn gave the ground a few more pats. "You should eat while the stew is hot."

Slowly, fearfully, Bright Rainbow approached. She took small steps and was poised to flee at the slightest hint of deception.

Evelyn sat perfectly still and smiled. She was tempted to lunge and grab hold once the girl was close enough, but she stifled the urge. To put her more at ease, she rambled, "Would you like to be my new friend? I would like to be yours. I did not have any sisters growing up and I always wanted one. Girls are easier to talk to than boys. My brother used to say I talk too much and would walk off when I bored him and . . ."

Bright Rainbow stopped and trembled and said in a tiny voice, "I had brothers."

Evelyn remembered the remains in the lodge.

"Two of them."

"I hope they were nicer to you than my brother was to me."

"They were nice, yes," Bright Rainbow said. "Fox Tail and Elk Running. It killed them. Both of them."

"What did?" Evelyn asked, although she knew full well.

"The Devil Cat."

"The what?"

"My people call it that. I thought my mother made it up. But it was real, as real as you and me."

"*Doyadukubichi*," Evelyn said, which was Shoshone for "mountain lion" or "cougar."

"*Kai*."

"No?"

"It is not a cat. It is a devil."

By then the girl was near enough for Evelyn to touch. "Have a seat and I will feed you."

Bright Rainbow folded her legs and delicately perched on her knees, her hands in her lap. She could not take her eyes off the bubbling stew.

"You have not eaten a meal in a while." Evelyn stated the obvious.

"No."

Evelyn heard the girl's stomach growl. She ladled stew into a tin cup and held it out. "I have plenty so eat as much as you want."

Bright Rainbow stared at the cup as if she had never seen one before. She tentatively went to wrap her hand around it.

"Be careful," Evelyn cautioned. "It is hot. Use the handle." She demonstrated how to hold it.

"A great thing," Bright Rainbow said. She tried a taste and her face lit with pleasure. "You are a good cook, Blue Flower."

"My mother is ten times as good. Her cakes make your mouth water and her bread is always delicious."

"My mother . . ." Bright Rainbow began, and her face clouded. She stopped and bit her lower lip and said, "I miss her. I cry and cry, I miss her so much."

Against her better judgment Evelyn asked, "What about your father? Did the Devil Cat get him, too?"

"He pushed me in a hole and . . ." Again Bright Rainbow stopped. Tears welled, and she bowed her head and spoke in a rush. "I saw him die. I saw him turn and stab at the cat with his spear and his knives and I think he cut it, too, but the cat was too big and too strong and it jumped on his chest and pinned him and tore at him with its teeth and its claws and he . . ." She stopped and shuddered.

Impulsivly, Evelyn threw her arm around the girl's frail shoulders and pulled her close. "Enough," she said. "Do not relive his death."

Bright Rainbow closed her eyes, set down the tin cup, and groaned. She uttered a loud sob and her whole body shook, and suddenly she was weeping in Evelyn's arms, her face pressed against Evelyn's dress. She cried and cried and cried and cried some more, and Evelyn held her and stroked her hair and patted her back and said over and over, "There, there." Bright Rainbow wept herself dry and finally stopped and sniffled and wiped her nose with her sleeve.

"I am sorry."

"For what?"

"I made you wet." Continuing to sniffle, Bright Rainbow pulled away and tucked her knees to her chest and wrapped her arms around her thin legs.

"It is nothing."

"I heard him scream."

"You do not need to tell me," Evelyn said.

"I saw the Devil Cat tear at him. I saw his blood. He tried not to cry out. He grit his teeth and the veins in his neck stood out and then he threw back his head and he screamed and screamed."

"Please stop."

Bright Rainbow quaked. "He looked at me and I saw how scared he was. Then he smiled."

"Oh God," Evelyn said in English.

"He smiled and he looked at me as he used to when he held me in his arms and told me that he loved me." Bright Rainbow pressed her face to her knees. "The cat bit his throat and that was the end." She wept some more, quietly, her hands clenched so hard, her knuckles were white.

Evelyn was patient with her. She hadn't lost her parents or her brother, but she had lost friends and others she cared for and keenly remembered her sorrow. She could imagine what the girl was going through.

On all sides of them the valley buzzed and chirped and chattered with life and vitality.

After a long interval Bright Rainbow sniffled and raised her head. Her cheeks glistened but her eyes were dry. "I am sorry."

"Stop saying that." Evelyn stroked her matted hair. "Finish your soup and then we'll talk some more."

Bright Rainbow ran her sleeve across her face, leaving a smear. She resumed eating, cradling the cup in both hands. She had eaten about half when she turned to Evelyn and said, "As soon as I am done we must leave."

"You are in no condition to ride," Evelyn said. She planned to clean the girl up and get more food into her and wait for her folks.

"We must," Bright Rainbow insisted.

"Finish your stew."

Bright Rainbow gripped Evelyn's arm. "You are not listening to me. Heed my words." She paused. "If we do not leave, we will die."

Chapter Fifteen

Degamawaku rode hard for the pass, climbing through thick timber. Ordinarily he would not push his horse so hard, but he was worried about Evelyn. He did not want to leave her alone. He did not want anything to happen to her.

Dega had never been in love before. He had liked some of the girls in his village, liked them a lot, but none had claimed his heart as Evelyn King had. She was all he thought about when he was not with her, all he dreamed about when he slept.

Dega hated that they had argued. He hated that his mother had caused a rift between them. But he didn't hold her at fault. His mother had been right; he did owe it to his people to do what he could to restore the Nansusequa to as they were. A terrible responsibility had been placed on his shoulders, and the weight was driving a wedge between Evelyn and him.

A tree limb materialized and Dega ducked. He concentrated on his riding. He would be the first to admit he was not a good rider, but then, the Nansusequas had never used horses. The first time he sat a horse was when Nate King gave them one as a gift.

Nate King. Now, there was a man Dega respected. For a while after the massacre of his people he had hated whites, hated all that they were and all that they stood for. Then he met the Kings. Evelyn had stirred him from the moment he set eyes on her, and her father had proven to be as considerate and decent as any Nansusequa ever born. As his people would say, Nate King had a good heart. So did Evelyn. Her brother, Zach, was different. Zach had a darkness about him, a passion for violence that burst from him as a stream burst its banks in a flood.

Dega had to swerve to avoid a boulder. Above him, and yet a long way off, was the pass. He craned his neck to try and see it but couldn't. He slapped his legs. His horse was lathered with sweat, but he didn't care. He would ride it to exhaustion if need be.

The slopes became steeper. Dega had to slow and didn't like it. The delay gnawed at him like a beaver gnawing at a tree.

Without warning the sorrel stumbled and nearly went down. Dega was almost pitched off. He grabbed the mane to keep from falling, and when the horse righted itself, he used his reins.

A hawk was circling high in the sky, but he paid it no mind. A doe dashed from a thicket, but he hardly glanced its way. His mind was on Evelyn and only on Evelyn.

The cliffs hove into sight, and Dega smiled. Soon he would be through them and then it was downhill to King Lake and their families. He hoped Nate was home and not off hunting. If that was the case, he would go to Zach. Now that he thought about it, he would go to Zach anyway and bring him back, too. Zach was as good a tracker as his father and much deadlier.

The sorrel slipped again. Dega patted and urged it on. A jay squawked at him and took wing. A marmot whistled a shrill warning and darted into its den.

The sorrel began to limp.

Dega looked down. He did not know a lot about horses, but he knew this was not good. He kept going in the hope it would stop limping, but instead the limp grew worse. Reluctantly, he drew rein and slid down. Squatting, he examined its front leg. Even to his untrained eye it was obvious the leg was swollen. He ran his hand up and down it as he had seen Nate King do and then lifted the hoof to inspect it. The hoof appeared to be fine. He set it down and unfurled and bit his lower lip. A long time ago Nate had told him that a horse with a limp should never be ridden. But he had no choice. There was Evelyn to think of. Accordingly, he climbed back on and goaded the sorrel higher.

The horse could barely walk.

Dega was in a quandary. He had to reach Nate quickly, but on foot it would take him the rest of the day and most of the night, and in the meantime, Evelyn was alone in that terrible valley.

The horse dipped with every step. Suddenly it stopped.

"Go," Dega said, and used the reins. The sorrel didn't move. He jabbed his heels as hard as he could and the sorrel turned its head and looked at him. "All right," Dega said, and climbed down. He glanced at the high cliffs and then back the way he had come.

He had a decision to make.

At a steady jog it would take him as long to reach Nate as it would to return to Evelyn.

Which should he do?

Dega frowned and took the reins and led the sorrel to a tree and tied it. Then, squaring his shoulders, he stared up the mountain at the pass.

"I wish we would go," Bright Rainbow said.

"I have explained why we are staying," Evelyn replied. She had hold of the girl's hand and was leading her toward the stream. The afternoon sun was warm on their backs, the high grass stirring in the breeze. "We have nothing to be afraid of."

A monarch butterfly flitted past and a grasshopper jumped from under their feet. In the woods a finch chirped.

"Yes," Bright Rainbow said, "we do."

Evelyn had been through this several times already. "I will protect you. I have my guns. And by morning my folks will be here."

"We should not stay the night."

Evelyn was tired of hearing that. They came to the bank and she nodded at a pool. "That will do. I'll turn my back and keep watch while you strip and jump in."

"I do not want to."

"You need a bath. Your hair is a mess and your dress is dirty. Wash it and wring it out and set it on the grass to dry while you clean yourself off."

Bright Rainbow faced her. "I will do as you ask. You are my new friend. But you make a mistake. I am young. I am not dumb. And I tell you now, Evelyn King. We should go while we can."

"Take your bath." Evelyn turned and walked a dozen steps. She could understand the girl's fear, but it was broad daylight and the mountain lion wasn't anywhere near or the other animals would be cowering in their thickets and nests. From where she stood she could see the length and breadth of the valley. True, the high grass might hide a skulking cat, but she was confident she would spot it before it rushed them. She heard splashing behind her.

"The water is cold, Blue Flower."

"Wash good," Evelyn said. "Especially your hair."

"You sound like my mother."

Evelyn smothered a laugh. "Tell me a little about yourself. How old are you?"

"I will have lived twelve winters this winter."

"Older than I thought," Evelyn said. The girl was small for her age. "Where are your nearest relatives? Grandparents or an aunt or an uncle?"

"My grandfather was bit by a rattlesnake when I was little. My grandmother took sick and died two winters ago. I have no aunts or uncles. There is only me."

"There must be someone." Evelyn reckoned that her mother would want to return the girl to her people. "A close friend of your mother's would do."

"Oh. I understand. You want to give me away."

"You need to be with your own kind, your own people."

"I like being with you."

"You hardly know me."

"I like being with you anyway."

"Get washed." Evelyn was annoyed at how stubborn the girl was. Idly gazing at the rocky crags to the north, she stiffened. For a split second she thought she saw a black form gliding down a high slope. It was there and then it wasn't. Given how far off it was and how big it must be, it had to have been a black bear. Black bears didn't worry her. Most fought shy of people.

"Blue Flower?" Bright Rainbow said.

"Are you washing?"

"Yes. I wanted to ask what we will do tonight."

"Stay put so Dega knows right where to find us."

"And if the Devil Cat comes?"

"I will shoot it."

"You will not see it, Blue Flower. You will not hear it. It is like a ghost, the Devil Cat."

"I'll keep a fire going. That will keep it away," Evelyn said. A fire kept most every animal at bay.

"We had a fire in our lodge and the Devil Cat came in after us."

"I will make the fire extra big. Now will you *please* wash?" Evelyn wriggled her foot in impatience. She looked to the north again. The bear had not reappeared. She imagined that by now Dega had reached the pass. Their spat notwithstanding, she could count on him not to let her down. Once her ma and pa arrived, all would be well.

The dark one was a shadow among shadows. His paws made no sound on the carpet of pine needles. His long body slung low, he stalked to a spur that overlooked the valley floor. He had come to this same spot on many an evening to watch and wait for prey. Cautiously, he raised his head and peered down at the pair below. His tail twitched and he bared his fangs, but he didn't growl. He must not give himself away.

One of the creatures was in the water. It was small, not much bigger than a fawn, except it stood on two legs and not four. The other was on the bank, watching. It was not much bigger. They would be easy kills, but instinct rooted him to the spur. Not in the daylight. He would wait for night. There was no hurry. He wasn't hungry.

The dark one lay and watched. He was curious about these creatures. They were different from everything else. They made so much noise, uttered so many strange sounds. They moved in ungainly steps, as slow as turtles. Yet they were dangerous. The hard thing he had stepped in had cost him part of his paw. The long sharp thing the male creature wielded had pierced his shoulder. He must be wary.

The small one was climbing out of the stream. She was clumsy. She slipped and fell back in and made a sharp bark. Again she tried, and stood on two legs and shook herself as the dark one did after a heavy rain. She picked up something lying on the grass and flapped it and then slipped it over her head and down around her thin body.

They were so strange, these creatures. The dark one saw the little one go to the bigger one and together they walked toward a clearing. A tingle ran through him. In the clearing stood one of the four-legged animals that looked like elk but weren't elk. He would enjoy feeding on its flesh.

Sliding back, the dark one wheeled and padded around the spur and into the trees. Every sense alert, he crept close enough to the clearing to see his quarry. They were sitting next to crackling spurts of red and orange.

The dark one flexed his claws. He had seen something similar in the den of the creatures he killed. It made him uneasy.

He fixed his attention on the little two-legs, studying them and their habits as he had studied deer when he was with his mother.

They were gibbering. Their noises were alien: high and low, slow and fast, clipped and flowing. Chipmunks and squirrels were noisy, too, but not to the degree the two-legs were.

His whiskers twitching, the dark one rested his chin on his leg. The sun was on its downward arc. Until it set he was content to lie there and observe.

Then he would make his kill.

Evelyn poured the last of the stew into the tin cup. "This is all there is," she said, marveling at the girl's appetite.

"Thank you," Bright Rainbow said. "I could not eat much more anyway."

"You are liable to burst," Evelyn teased. She set the pot down and leaned against her saddle. "A good night's rest and you'll be as frisky as a colt come morning."

"If we are alive."

"You chew at a bone until there is nothing left."

"I do not eat bones."

Evelyn laughed. "That is a white expression." She picked up the Hawken and the pot and stood. "You finish eating. I will be right back. I am going to wash this."

"Do not leave me alone."

"I am only going to the stream. I can see you from there." Evelyn turned to go and the girl jumped up.

"Take me with you."

Evelyn shrugged. "If you want. But you will be fine here."

Bright Rainbow quickly scooted to her side. "I never want to be alone again," she said.

Evelyn strolled into the high grass. To the west the sun was going down and the sky was streaked with pink, red, and yellow. "It will be dark soon," she mentioned.

"That is when the Devil Cat will come."

"How many times must I tell you? Mountain lions don't stay put in one spot. They thin out the game and move on."

"What if there is a lot of game?"

Evelyn had to remind herself to go easy with her. "When was the last time you saw the Devil Cat?"

"When my father was killed."

"Then what are you worried about? Besides, we'll have a fire. We'll see it if it tries to sneak up on us."

"The fire will not help. The Devil Cat is not like other cats. You cannot see it in the dark."

"Why not?"

"The Devil Cat is black."

Evelyn stopped cold in her tracks. She remembered the black animal she took for a black bear. "Surely not," she said out loud.

"What?" Bright Rainbow asked.

"Nothing," Evelyn said. But a seed of worry took root.

Chapter Sixteen

Nighttime in the Rocky Mountains. The temperature dropped and the wind bent the treetops. It was the second night of the full moon, and with the moon's rising a cacophony of bestial roars and howls ripped the wilds. A lady from the East once told Evelyn that it sounded like hell unleashed. Ordinarily, the dark and the wind and the cries hardly bothered her—when she was safe and snug in the family's cabin. But to be out in the bedlam, to be sitting by a fire in a small ring of light in the middle of all that vast black sea of savagery, to be alone except for the company of a little girl while a legion of meat-eaters prowled and slew and yowled, was enough to raise goose bumps on Evelyn's skin and for her to keep the Hawken in her lap and a hand on one of her pistols.

The whites of Bright Rainbow's eyes were showing as she nibbled at a piece of pemmican. She raised her head at every nearby yip and bleat. "The Devil Cat is out there. I know it."

"Will you stop?" Evelyn was tired of hearing about it. She had been worried about the black animal she saw all afternoon and evening, but it had not bothered them.

"We should have gone to my hole," Bright Rainbow said. "It is under a boulder and there is room for two."

"How is it the Devil Cat did not go in after you?"

"I do not know," Bright Rainbow said. "Maybe it did not see my father push me in."

"We do not need to hide in your hole. I will not let anything happen to you," Evelyn vowed.

"My father always said the same."

Evelyn helped herself to pemmican. She imagined that by now Dega had reached her parents and they were flying to help her. The thought put her a little more at ease.

Bright Rainbow went to take another bite. "Look!" she whispered, and pointed.

Eyes were staring at them from the woods. Evelyn started to snap the Hawken to her shoulder and stopped. The eyes were small and round, not big and slanted. "A deer, I think."

Neither of them moved. The eyes blinked a few times and melted into the vegetation.

"See?" Evelyn said.

Bright Rainbow let out a long breath. "I was scared."

"You have to stop doing that to yourself," Evelyn advised. "How about if we do something to take your mind off the cat?"

"What?"

Evelyn hadn't brought cards or a book. "We could tell stories. I was on a buffalo hunt not long ago and scalp hunters came after us." She stopped. On second thought, that was almost as frightening as talking about the cat.

"Scalphunters?"

"They take hair for money." Evelyn bit into the pemmican, sorry she had brought it up. She chewed, and suddenly stopped in midbite. Another pair of eyes was staring at them—or *glaring* rather. Big eyes. Slanted eyes. "No," she said softly.

"What is wrong?" Bright Rainbow turned, and gasped. Dropping her pemmican, she scuttled to Evelyn's side and gripped her arm. "The Devil Cat! It must be."

"It could be any mountain lion or a bobcat," Evelyn said, trying to set her at ease. But the eyes were too big for a bobcat, and the odds of another mountain lion having the same range as the one that killed the girl's family were slim.

"It is the Devil Cat," Bright Rainbow insisted in stark fright. She dug her fingers into Evelyn's arm. "We must flee."

Evelyn glanced at Buttercup. She would have to turn her back to the cat to throw on the saddle, and she wasn't about to do that. "We will sit still. It is bound to go away."

Bright Rainbow whimpered.

The eyes went on glaring.

Evelyn shifted uneasily. She considered shooting. She might hit it. Then again, she might not, and if she only wounded it, it might attack.

"What is it waiting for?"

"Hush." Evelyn grasped the unlit end of a burning brand and stood. Holding it aloft, she took several steps toward the eyes. They stayed where they were.

"Don't!" Bright Rainbow pleaded.

"Stay put," Evelyn commanded, and darting forward, she hurled the brand. It landed short of the woods. Instantly, the grass caught and flared, casting light several feet but not far enough to reveal the cat. In a flash the eyes were gone. Evelyn ran over, but beyond the fading light was ink black save for patches where moonbeams penetrated the canopy. Thwarted, she stamped out the flames before they spread and ignited the woods.

Bright Rainbow was only a few feet away. "You scared it off!" she exclaimed in awe.

"The fire did." Evelyn clasped the girl's hand and backed away from the trees.

"You are very brave to do what you did."

"Fire nearly always scares an animal off."

"I was afraid," Bright Rainbow said.

"So was I," Evelyn confessed. She bid the girl sit and added limbs to the fire so it blazed higher. It would be a long night, she reflected. She didn't dare fall asleep or the fire would die and the cat would be on them. She decided to put coffee on, only that required more water.

"Listen," Bright Rainbow said.

The valley had fallen quiet. From off over the peaks came a few howls, but the valley itself was eerily still.

"Everything is scared of the Devil Cat."

That was preposterous, but Evelyn didn't say so. "I have to go to the stream."

"Now?" Bright Rainbow clutched her arm "I will go with you."

Arguing would be pointless. Evelyn chose another brand and gave it to her, as well as the pot, so her hands were free to hold the Hawken. "Stay close."

"As close as your skin."

Bright Rainbow wasn't exaggerating; she rubbed against Evelyn with every step. When Evelyn stopped to listen, the girl bumped into her.

"Watch where you are walking."

"If I could I would climb on your back."

The grass, and the darkness, closed around them. As high as Evelyn's waist, the grass swayed and rustled with the gusts of wind. The brand lit them and not much else.

Evelyn inched forward. When she realized it would take half the night at the rate she was going, she walked faster. She never stopped glancing to each side and behind her.

Bright Rainbow was trembling. When something burst from their path she cried out in panic and recoiled, and might have run off if Evelyn's hadn't grabbed her.

"It was a rabbit."

"I thought . . ." Bright Rainbow said, and did not go on.

"Stay calm."

"You would not say that if you had seen the Devil Cat," Bright Rainbow said. "You would not say that if you saw it kill your father and mother and brother."

"Try," Evelyn said.

From somewhere in the grass came a guttural cough.

Evelyn's breath caught in her throat. She had heard similar coughs before; it was the sound of a large cat. Apparently the beast didn't care that they knew it was there. She advanced on the balls of her feet, poised to fight or flee. Not that she would run off and leave Bright Rainbow. Her father and mother had instilled in her that when people were in trouble, she should help. She would protect the girl with her dying breath, if need be.

There was another cough but from a different spot.

"Blue Flower," Bright Rainbow whispered, and extended a quaking finger. "Do you see them?"

Deep in the grass, eyes gleamed in the flickering light of the brand.

Evelyn jerked a pistol. The rifle was more powerful and could drop bigger game, but she preferred to save it for when she truly needed it. She thumbed back the flintlock's hammer and set the trigger and took deliberate aim—just as the eyes vanished. She fired anyway. The pistol boomed and spat smoke and lead. Nothing happened. There were no shrieks of pain, no sign that she had hit it.

Bright Rainbow dropped to her knees and wrapped an arm around Evelyn's leg. "Do not let it kill us."

"Get up," Evelyn said. She jammed the spent pistol under her belt. Suddenly pain seared her leg. Bright Rainbow had held the brand too close. "Get up," she said again, and pulled her to her feet.

"We should go back."

"No." Evelyn needed the coffee to stay awake. Alert for eye shine and bent at the waist so she could see into the grass, she came to the bank. Normally the gurgle of the water would delight her, but now it made her uneasy; it would be harder to hear the mountain lion. "Fill the pot. Hurry."

Bright Rainbow moved to where the bank sloped, and stopped. "I cannot do it."

"I will protect you."

Her Adam's apple bobbing, Bright Rainbow hopped down. She quickly squatted and dipped the pot in the stream. With her other hand she held the brand high over her head.

Evelyn gave a start. The brand was burning low.

They would be lucky to make it to the clearing before it went out. "How much water do you have?"

Bring Rainbow raised the pot and shook it. "Only half."

"That will have to do. Climb back up." Evelyn reached down to help her—and her heart seemed to stop in her chest. Across the stream, in the grass on the other side, the slanted eyes had reappeared, fixed intently on her and the little Sheepeater. She tucked the Hawken to her shoulder but didn't fire. She wanted a clear shot.

"What is it?" Bright Rainbow asked, and looked in the direction Evelyn was looking. Uttering a squeal of terror, she scrambled up the bank. "Kill it!" she cried, slipping behind her.

"I need to be sure," Evelyn said. She blinked, and the eyes weren't there. Suspecting that the cat was circling them, she shifted to either side but saw no trace of it. "Go slow," she cautioned.

"I can feel its eyes on us."

So could Evelyn. She put each foot behind her with care so she didn't stumble. Any mistake now, however slight, could cost them their lives. It took forever to reach the clearing. The brand was nearly out. The fire itself was low but still burning. She moved toward it, intending to add firewood.

A living lightning bolt streaked out of the trees and launched itself at Buttercup—a black lightning bolt.

Evelyn barely had time to bring the Hawken up when the Devil Cat leaped and landed on Buttercup's back. Buttercup whinnied and sought to rear, but the picket rope hampered her. The cat, about to bite at her neck, was unbalanced and nearly fell off.

Evelyn saw it clearly for the first time. God help her, but it was exactly as Bright Rainbow had described: a huge cat as black as the bottom of a well with eyes that blazed with ferocity.

"Kill it!" Bright Rainbow yelled.

Evelyn was trying to fix a bead, but Buttercup, bucking and kicking and turning, was doing all she could to throw the cat off, and the cat was never still. Its neck filled her sights, only to be replaced the next instant by its tail.

Bright Rainbow tugged at Evelyn's dress. "What are you waiting for?"

Buttercup was frantically pulling at the rope. Already her flanks were red with blood. The mountain lion snapped at her throat and ripped out a chunk of hide. Squealing, Buttercup reared, the picket stake pulled free, and she flew toward the forest.

Evelyn lunged for the rope, but the horse was moving too fast.

Buttercup raced into the trees, the mountain lion clawing and tearing. By happenstance Buttercup passed under an oak and a low limb raked her back and caught the cat across the chest. With a piercing yowl the mountain lion went tumbling and Buttercup disappeared into the darkness.

Evelyn was rooted in dismay. She'd had the buttermilk for years and adored the animal. Then she realized she shouldn't be worried about the horse; she should be worried about them. Whirling, she added fuel to the fire and yanked Bright Rainbow down beside her.

"What do we do?" the girl asked.

"We stay put."

"Is that wise?"

"Yes." The way Evelyn saw it, the fire was still their best defense. She realized she had made a grave mistake in not leaving when they had the chance. Now they were stranded afoot, the worst fate that could befall them.

From the woods came a shrill shriek.

"The Devil Cat is mad," Bright Rainbow said.

"I aim to make it madder if it comes anywhere near us." Evelyn commenced to reload her spent pistol. She would need all three guns to stop a mountain lion that size, and even they might not be enough.

"We will still wait for your parents?"

"We are not budging," Evelyn confirmed.

"I hope you know what you are doing."

So did Evelyn.

Bright Rainbow anxiously regarded the wall of vegetation. "Why did the Devil Cat go after your horse and not us?"

"Who can say?" Evelyn said.

"One thing I know. We are next," Bright Rainbow said.

Evelyn slid the ramrod from its housing under the barrel. "Yes," she agreed. "We are."

Chapter Seventeen

The fire roared, the flames two feet high. Its comforting light lit the entire clearing and the fringe of woodland.

Evelyn sat with her knees tucked to her chest and the Hawken propped between her legs. Next to her, curled in a ball and sound asleep, was Bright Rainbow. Evelyn refilled her coffee cup and glanced at the firewood they had left. She frowned. It wasn't enough to last the rest of the night.

Hours had passed since the Devil Cat attacked Buttercup. There had been no sign of it since. Evelyn hoped—she prayed—the mountain lion had been hurt when the tree limb struck it. Hurt so badly, it had gone off to its lair and would leave them be.

By her reckoning it was past three in the morning. Another three hours, or so, and the sun would be up. Another three hours and her parents would be there. She was a little surprised they weren't there already. She'd figured her father would ride like a madman to her rescue. She gazed along the dark funnel of the valley as she had a dozen times since she sat down and did more praying.

"Where are you?" Evelyn wondered out loud. The only reason she could think of for them not to show was that something had happened to Dega and he never got to them. The prospect terrified her.

Evelyn sipped more coffee. There was about a

cupful left in the pot, and that was all. So far it had kept her awake and alert, but she could feel fatigue nipping at her mind and body and every so often she stifled a yawn. She envied Bright Rainbow being able to sleep. The girl had tried to stay awake and help keep watch, but exhaustion and a full belly refused to be denied.

Down out of the moonlit peaks to the west drifted the howl of a wolf. She had heard an awful lot of wolves that night, many more than usual. She speculated on whether a new pack was roaming that region. The notion didn't scare her. She wasn't afraid of wolves as she was of grizzlies and mountain lions. When she was little, her brother had a pet wolf for a while, and she had liked the frisky fellow considerably. She gazed up at the beautiful full moon and almost felt like howling herself. Grinning at her silliness, she raised the tin cup to her lips—and her heart skipped a beat.

The eyes were back, across the clearing at the edge of the trees, aglow with reflected light from the fire, unblinking in their intensity.

Evelyn set down the cup and took up the Hawken. She thumbed back the hammer and set the rear trigger so that all it would take was a slight squeeze on the front trigger to fire. Her Hawken had a maple stock with a curve in the wood for her cheek. She put her cheek to the curve and sighted down the barrel.

The eyes vanished.

Evelyn held the rifle to her cheek until her arms couldn't take the strain, and lowered it. If she didn't know better she would think the mountain lion was toying with them. All she wanted was a clear shot, just one clear shot, and their ordeal would be over.

The flames were dwindling. She added one to the three pieces of a broken limb they had left and tried not to think of what she must do after she added the other two. To take her mind off it she sipped coffee and thought about Dega and how her picnic had turned into a disaster. So much for being alone with him. So much for sharing her heart and having him share his.

Bright Rainbow groaned and stirred and muttered in her sleep. Her arms and legs twitched. She was in the grip of a dream or more likely a nightmare because she started to mew in terror and uttered a soft sob.

Evelyn shook her.

The girl's eyes snapped open and she sat bolt upright. She looked around in confusion and then at the fire and at Evelyn. Sweat caked her face and she was as pale as a bedsheet.

"Are you all right?"

"I had a bad dream."

"The Devil Cat?"

"Yes." Bright Rainbow scanned the impenetrable wall of forest. "Have you seen it?"

"No," Evelyn lied.

"Maybe it is gone."

Evelyn bobbed her head at their meager firewood. "I have to gather more or the fire will go out."

"I will help," Bright Rainbow offered.

"It is safer for you here."

"I am too afraid to be alone. I will carry a burning stick so you can see."

Evelyn would have her hands full with her rifle and the firewood. She couldn't hold a torch, too. "If

I agree, you are to do exactly as I say. If I tell you to run, you run."

"I will not leave you. I would rather die than be alone again."

"Enough of that kind of talk." Evelyn slid her hunting knife from its sheath. "To protect yourself with. Go for the eyes."

The girl took it and lightly pricked her finger with the tip and ran the same finger along the edge. "It is very sharp."

"A dull knife doesn't do much good." Evelyn rose. "We should go while the flames are still high."

Bright Rainbow chose a brand. She held it out in front of her and clenched the knife tight. "I am ready."

The forest was ominously silent.

Her skin rippling with dread, Evelyn crossed to the woods. Bright Rainbow's arm rubbed her with every step. She spotted a downed limb, but it was too thick for her to break apart. Stepping over it, she went around a pine. The brand hissed and gave off smoke that tingled her nose. "Try not to hold that so close to my face."

"Sorry."

Evelyn roved past a thicket wide enough to hide the mountain lion. She kept the Hawken leveled, just in case.

"The Devil Cat is near," Bright Rainbow whispered breathlessly. "I can feel him."

Evelyn told her to be quiet. But she could feel the cat's presence, too. She looked for eye shine.

"There," Bright Rainbow said, and pointed with the knife. "Plenty of firewood."

Fallen limbs littered the ground at the base of a

dead tree. Evelyn stooped to grab one and a growl rumbled out of the darkness. Straightening, she jammed the Hawken to her shoulder. "Where is it?" The growl had seemed to come from everywhere at once.

"I do not know." Bright Rainbow's voice quaked with terror. "We should go back."

"We need the wood." Evelyn hastily scooped up several pieces of a thick limb and turned to retrace their steps.

The eyes were behind them. The mountain lion was between them and the clearing. It couldn't have been more than twenty feet away.

"God, no," Evelyn said. She dropped the firewood and snapped the Hawken to her cheek. "I have you now." She fired. At the boom of the shot the eyes rose straight into the air and came down again, and blinked out. Drawing a flintlock, Evelyn shouted, "Stay by my side!" and charged forward. She came to the spot where she thought the eyes had been and cast about for sign and found it in the form of bright scarlet drops on the grass and the leaves. "I hit it!" she exulted.

"But where did it go?"

Evelyn turned in a complete circle. "I don't know." She had hit it, yes, but there wasn't much blood, which might mean she'd only nicked it. And a wounded meat-eater was always more dangerous. Her father had warned her of that since she was old enough to hold a gun.

A snarl rent the air.

Evelyn spun but saw only dark undergrowth and trees. With its black coat, the mountain lion was practically invisible. It could spring at them at any moment. "We're going back," she declared, and retreated toward the clearing.

"What about the firewood?"

"Leave it," Evelyn said. Their lives weren't worth the risk. She was relieved when they emerged into the open but not so happy at how low the fire had burned. Another ten minutes or so and it would go out, plunging them in darkness and leaving them vulnerable.

"I am scared," Bright Rainbow said.

So was Evelyn, but as her father always impressed on her, she was a King and the Kings never gave up. Where there was a will, there was a way, he liked to say. She stood with her back to the fire and commenced to reload her rifle.

Bright Rainbow cast the brand into the fire and gripped the hilt of the knife in her small hands. "The Devil Cat will kill us."

"Stop talking like that." Evelyn was trying to load and watch the woods at the same time, and she spilled some powder.

"There is only one safe place. The hole where I hid after it killed my father."

"No." Evelyn felt the best place to make their stand was in the open where they could see the mountain lion coming and have room to move.

"It is big enough for both of us."

"No, I said."

"You can kill the Devil Cat if it tries to crawl in after us."

Without thinking Evelyn snapped, "Did you listen to your mother as poorly as you listen to me?"

Bright Rainbow's scarecrow frame slumped in sorrow. "I always did as my mother asked."

"Then do the same with me."

"You are not my mother," Bright Rainbow said, and with that, she snatched another brand from the fire, whirled, and ran toward the forest.

"Get back here!" Evelyn hollered, but the girl ignored her and plunged into the Stygian mire.

Evelyn raced after her, fully aware of the mistake they were making. "Come back!" she tried again.

As fleet as an antelope, Bright Rainbow didn't heed. The burning brand rose and dipped and weaved right and left as she avoided obstacles.

"Please!" Evelyn reckoned the girl was trying to reach her hidey-hole before the torch went out. Something compelled her to look over her shoulder, and her breath caught in her throat. A black blur was crossing the clearing in a beeline after them. The mountain lion had given chase.

Fear clutched at Evelyn's heart. The cat could see in the dark and she couldn't. It would catch up and spring on her. She ran another dozen strides and stopped and spun. Better to face it, she reasoned, than have it take her from behind. She never heard a sound, yet suddenly there it was, a darker black than the night itself, its eyes glinting in the starlight. Evelyn swallowed and brought the Hawken up just as the mountain lion sprang. She had no time to cock it. A heavy blow to her left shoulder spun her halfway around and pain spiked her body clear down to her toes. A raking forepaw had slashed her. She turned to confront the beast, but the mountain lion hadn't stopped.

It was after Bright Rainbow.

"No!" Evelyn cried, and sprinted madly to the girl's aid. She didn't shoot. She couldn't hold the rifle steady enough to be sure of bringing the mountain lion down. "Bright Rainbow!" she screamed. "Look out!"

The girl heard her—and stopped. She raised the brand just as an ebony form arced through the air. She was smashed to the ground and the burning brand fell next to her.

"Noooooo!" Evelyn hurtled forward. She saw the mountain lion straddling Bright Rainbow, saw the girl frozen in dread. Suddenly stopping, Evelyn sighted down the barrel, and fired. She rushed the shot, but she scored; blood spurted from the monster cat's flank. With an unearthly screech, the mountain lion spun toward her, its tail flailing like a whip. She thought it was going to charge her, but instead it wheeled and bounded into the undergrowth.

Bright Rainbow didn't move.

In a spurt of speed Evelyn reached her. The girl's eyes were closed and blood oozed from half a dozen slash marks. Evelyn dropped to a knee. "Bright Rainbow?"

She showed no signs of life.

Evelyn gripped her arm and shook. "Bright Rainbow? Answer me."

The girl's eyes opened, twin mirrors of utter and total fear. She trembled and whimpered.

Evelyn shook her harder. "Snap out of it! We must run or the cat will get us both."

Bright Rainbow's eyes weren't on Evelyn; they were fixed blankly on the heavens. Tears trickled from their corners.

"Listen to me!" Evelyn demanded, and when that got no reaction, she slapped her.

A sharp intake of breath, and Bright Rainbow

calmed. She pressed a hand to her cheek and said in a tiny voice, "You hit me."

"I'll do it again if you don't get up. How badly are you hurt?"

"I was clawed a little," the girl said.

Evelyn pulled her to her feet. "This hole of yours. How far is it?"

"We are close."

The brand was almost out. Evelyn grabbed it and held it higher so the breeze lent the flames new life. "Take me. Hurry. And carry this for me." She shoved the Hawken at her. There was no time to reload. She drew a pistol.

Bright Rainbow just stood there. "My mother never hit me."

"I am not your mother. I am your friend. And I am trying to keep us both alive." Evelyn pushed her. "Now *run*."

"Friends do not hit friends," Bright Rainbow said, but she turned and made off through the pines and spruce and scattered oaks. She was limping.

"What is wrong with your leg?"

"I twisted my ankle when the Devil Cat jumped on me."

"Stop calling it that. It is a mountain lion. A black mountain lion but only a mountain lion. It can be killed like any other."

"You are wrong, Blue Flower. My father stabbed it and it did not die. You have shot it with your thunderstick and it did not die. The Devil Cat cannot be hurt like we can."

"I made it bleed. And anything that bleeds can die. Now hush and get us there." Evelyn needed to listen for the painter. Not that she would hear it if it didn't want her to. She remembered to cock the flintlock. As heavy as it was, she held it in both hands.

Bright Rainbow's "not far" turned out to be a quarter of a mile. Every step was an agony of suspense. Evelyn never knew but when a heavy body would smash into her and fangs and claws would rip and rend. The forest thinned and ended, and above was a slope covered by a jumble of rocks and boulders. Bright Rainbow headed for the largest boulder. She stopped and pointed. At its base was a dark cavity not much wider than she was.

"There."

"Inside. Hurry." Evelyn faced down the mountain. The brand was almost out. Its light barely reached the trees, but it was enough; two malevolent eyes stared up at her.

From out of the hole came a muffled "I am in."

Evelyn crouched and leaned the brand against a rock. She went to all fours and scrambled backward, sliding her feet and then her legs into the hole and easing the rest of her after. The blazing eyes swept toward her. She levered her elbows and found herself in a dank hole barely long enough and wide enough for her and the girl both. They were pressed close together. She could move her arms but little else. She trained the muzzle on the opening and waited.

From outside came a growl. A shadow passed across the hole, but the mountain lion didn't look in.

Evelyn prayed it would so she could send a ball crashing into its brain. Suddenly the light faded. The brand had gone out. Tense with apprehension, she held the flintlock steady. But the mountain lion was either too shrewd or too wary to try to get at them. Nothing happened, and after a while she wondered if it was out there.

"Blue Flower?" Bright Rainbow whispered.

"Not now."

"Thank you," Bright Rainbow said quietly.

Evelyn looked at her. "You are welcome. Now be still." She focused on the opening and only the opening. No sounds drifted in save now and then the faraway yip of a coyote. Her shoulders ached and her arms grew weary from holding the pistol. Over an hour had gone by when she let the muzzle dip and winced at the pain in her shoulders. "I think it has gone." She broke their long silence.

"Or it is waiting for us to crawl out."

"That could be," Evelyn admitted. "Which is why we are staying put until daylight."

"I will do whatever you ask of me," Bright Rainbow said.

Something in the girl's voice prompted Evelyn to ask, "Are you all right?"

"I am tired and dizzy."

"Dizzy?" Evelyn repeated. "Why?"

"Maybe from all the blood."

"Your side wasn't bleeding that badly," Evelyn recollected.

"Not my side, my back. The Devil Cat clawed me there, too, as I fell. I think its claws went deep."

"Let me see." Evelyn slid her hand over the dirt and groped the girl's arm and shoulder and slid it down her back. She felt rips in the buckskin, and her questing fingers brushed deep cuts. The cat's claws had gone in an inch or more. She pried at the dress and realized it was soaked. "Why didn't you say something sooner?"

"We had to get in here or it would hurt you, too."

"Consarn you," Evelyn said in English.

"It hurts."

Evelyn eased her hand out and wiped it on her dress. The smell of fresh blood mixed with the scent of the dirt. "There is nothing I can do until morning."

"I understand."

Evelyn bit her lower lip. The girl needed stitching. Worse, if dirt got into the wounds, they might become infected. "Let me know if you start to feel worse."

There was no answer.

"Bright Rainbow?"

"I am sleepy."

Evelyn touched the girl's cheek. It was as cold as ice. She tried to remember everything her mother had told her about flesh wounds. Where *was* her mother? Why weren't her parents there yet? Dega had had plenty of time to get to King Valley and come back. She debated leaving their sanctuary so she could tend to Bright Rainbow's wounds, but it would be folly with the black beast lurking close by. "I hate this," she said out loud. She figured it couldn't be long until daybreak. If only the girl could last that long.

The minutes were eternities. Evelyn's eyelids grew heavy and twice her chin drooped, but each time she jerked her head up and shook the need to sleep away. She was terribly uncomfortable and her body became stiff and cold. She could only imagine how much worse Bright Rainbow must feel.

In the woods below a finch warbled.

Evelyn perked her ears. Birds always greeted the new day with a chorus of cries, and sure enough, the finch's warble was the signal for dozens more to break into song and for jays to utter raucous shrieks. Holding the pistol in front of her, she edged to the opening. To the east a pink tinge marked the break of the new day. Below, the slope was empty. Shadow shrouded the forest. The mountain lion was gone. Or it could be that that was what it wanted her to think. Regardless, she wriggled out of the hole and onto her knees. Her legs were so stiff she could hardly move them.

One eye on the forest, Evelyn reached back in for the Hawken. She hurriedly reloaded and slid the pistol under her belt. Now came the dangerous part. Setting the rifle down, she poked her arms and head into the hole and took hold of the little Tukaduka. "Bright Rainbow?"

The girl didn't stir.

"Bright Rainbow, can you hear me?" Evelyn shook her. When that failed to provoke a reply, she bunched her shoulders and pulled. It took some doing. She had to tug and twist, but she got the girl out and laid her on her back. "Bright Rainbow?" She moved her chin back and forth. All the girl did was groan.

Evelyn would never know what made her look over her shoulder. Some sixth sense, maybe. The sight of the black mountain lion slinking silently toward her with its chin practically brushing the ground sent her blood to racing. Its fiery eyes locked on hers. Mesmerized, she couldn't move. She saw its paws flex, and then, with a scream that set her neck hairs to prickling, it launched itself at her. She grabbed for the

Hawken but got hold of it by the barrel and not the stock. In self-preservation she swung with all her strength.

Struck full in the face, the mountain lion fell onto all fours. Evelyn staggered against the boulder. The lion snarled and crouched to spring, and she raised her rifle to swing again. For a span of heartbeats they were statues—and then there was a buzz and a *thwunk* and the mountain lion leaped into the air with a feathered shaft jutting from its side. It landed and spun and screeched in rage. A second shaft missed it by the width of one of its whiskers. With another earsplitting scream, it bounded toward the trees.

Up the slope ran a figure clad in green. He had another shaft nocked and raised his bow, but the cat gained cover before he could let fly. He stopped a few feet from Evelyn and gave her a look of such worry and devotion, her heart melted.

"Dega!"

"Evelyn." Dega opened his arms and she stepped into them. For a moment he forgot about the cat and the girl at their feet. His joy was boundless. He had run all through the night, driving himself to the point of exhaustion and beyond. His legs were welters of torment and his lungs hurt with every breath.

Evelyn stepped back. "Where are my father and mother?"

Dega told her about his horse, and how he'd had a decision to make: continue on foot and not get back to her until much later than she expected or return to help her get the girl to King Valley. "I hope you not mad," he said breathlessly. "I come back to you."

"Mad?" Evelyn said, and couldn't say any more for the constriction in her throat. She saw that his buckskins were drenched and that he was red in the face, and panting. "You big lunkhead. Why would I be mad?"

Dega was shocked. A lunkhead, Shakespeare McNair had told him, was someone who had, as McNair put it, "rocks between their ears." Implying they were stupid. "I have rocks in head?"

"What? Oh, no, no, no." Evelyn forgot herself and kissed him on the neck and the cheek. "You did exactly right."

Dega thought his chest would explode. All night he had thought about how much he cared for her. All night he had been thinking about their argument and his mother, and he had come to a decision. "I want you know, our children be Nansusequa and white."

"Oh, Dega." Evelyn woud have lavished more kisses on him, but just then Bright Rainbow groaned Bending, she slid her arms under her and picked her up. "We have to get her to the clearing. Guard me."

Dega would die for her if he had to. That was another conclusion he had come to. When they go home he would sit down with his mother and explain his feelings. She had always been so caring and considerate, he was sure she would understand

Bright Rainbow weighed more than Evelyn reckoned. Huffing, she got her to the bottom of the slope and merged with the woods. The sky had brightened and the shadows were dispersing.

Dega trailed her, protecting her, the bowstring pulled back, ready to loose a shaft at the first sign o the black mountain lion.

Evelyn tripped over an exposed root and firmed her hold on Bright Rainbow. A lot of birds were still singing. A rose-red grosbeak with black wings and a black tail flew over them, its brown mate at its side. She skirted several alders and spied the clearing and turned her head to tell Dega just as a sable pattering ram launched itself out of a thicket and slammed into him from the side. She screamed his name and bent to deposit the girl.

Dega had caught movement out of the corner of his eye and tried to turn, but he wasn't quick enough. Pain shot up his arm and along his side, and he was knocked against a pine and fell. Suddenly he was face-to-snarling-face with the cat, its forepaws on his chests, its fangs gaping wide to close on his throat. He jammed the bow into its mouth and razors opened his fingers. Before he could draw his hand away, the cat bit down. The pain was more than he could bear, and he cried out.

In fear for Dega's life, Evelyn fired from the hip. At that range she couldn't miss; the slug cored the lion's side. In a flash the cat spun and was on her, slashing in a fury. She retreated and her heel caught on Bright Rainbow and down she sprawled.

Dega's left hand was useless. The cat had bitten clean through it. He drew his knife, and as the beast pounced on Evelyn, he dived and stabbed, seeking to turn it from her so it would attack him. He succeeded; it did.

Evelyn's senses reeled from a blow to the head. Her dress was torn and she was bleeding, but all that mattered to her was the sight of Dega on the ground with the black mountain lion tearing at him in a frenzy. Clutching her flintlocks, she thumbed back both hammers as she drew. Dega was stabbing and the mountain lion was biting and clawing. She threw herself full length and rammed both muzzle against the mountain lion's head. The cat started to rise and turn toward her. She fired both pistols a once.

The black mountain lion arched its face to the sky Only half was left, and the lone eye seemed to fix on the moon. It yowled and collapsed.

In the silence that followed, Evelyn rose on un steady legs. The cat had fallen across Dega and nei ther was moving. "Dega?" She pushed, but the mountain lion was too heavy. "Dega, talk to me."

"What you want me say?"

"You're alive!"

"I think so."

Evelyn laughed giddily. She pushed, and Dega pushed, and together they rolled the black beast off. Grimacing, he sat up and looked down at him self. His green buckskin shirt and pants were shred ded, and he had been sliced and cut all over.

"You're bleeding." Evelyn stated the obvious. So was she.

"I live." Dega got his moccasins under him, and stood. "I help you."

It took the two of them to carry Bright Rainbow the rest of the way. They placed her near the ember and Evelyn rekindled the fire. She was weak and strangely sluggish yet elated to be breathing. "How are you holding up?"

Since all Dega had in his hands was his knife and it wasn't at all heavy, he said, "I holding fine."

A rumbling like thunder drew Evelyn's gaze down the valley. Two riders were galloping toward them, and one of the riders was leading a butter-milk. "Ma and Pa and Buttercup!" she exclaimed.

Dega grunted. "I forget tell you. I see your horse. It run by me. I try to catch but it faster than my feet."

"Buttercup must have gone all the way home and they started out after us right away," Evelyn de-duced. "Pa must have tracked us by torchlight most of the night." She clasped her hands and laughed for joy. "Everything will be all right. Ma is good at heal-ing. She'll help us and have Bright Rainbow on the mend in no time. Isn't that great?"

Dega remembered an expression her brother liked to use. He hoped it fit the occasion. "Just dandy," he said.

Author's Note

This entry in the King saga was taken from Evelyn King's diary and not her father's journals. Nate makes mention of the affair but only briefly.

Evelyn is quite insistent that the mountain lion was black. Current scientific opinion has it that black mountain lions do not exist. Yet there have been scores of eyewitness accounts of such cats.

The reader is left to decide whether her tale is true. It should be noted that many years later, an old, moth-eaten black cat hide said to belong to the King family was sold at auction in Estes Park. No one knows where that hide is today.

INTERACT WITH DORCHESTER ONLINE!

Want to learn more about your favorite books and authors?
Want to talk with other readers that like to read the same books as you?
Want to see up-to-the-minute Dorchester news?

VISIT DORCHESTER AT:
DorchesterPub.com
Twitter.com/DorchesterPub
Facebook.com (Search Pages)

DISCUSS DORCHESTER'S NOVELS AT:
Dorchester Forums at DorchesterPub.com
GoodReads.com
LibraryThing.com
Myspace.com/books
Shelfari.com
WeRead.com

COVERING THE OLD WEST FROM COVER TO COVER.

Since 1953 we have been helping preserve the American West with great original photos, true stories, new facts, old facts and current events.

True West Magazine
We Make the Old West Addictive.

Bill Pronzini &
Marcia Muller

The dark clouds are gathering, and it's promising to be a
doozy of a storm at the River Bend stage station ... where
the owners are anxiously awaiting the return of their missing
daughter. Where a young cowboy hopes to find safety from
the rancher whose wife he's run away with. Where a Pinker-
ton agent has tracked the quarry he's been chasing for years.
Thunder won't be the only thing exploding along ...

CRUCIFIXION RIVER

Bill Pronzini and Marcia Muller are a husband-wife writ-
ing team with numerous individual honors, including the
Lifetime Achievement Award from the Private Eye Writers
of America, the Grand Master Award from Mystery Writers
of America, and the American Mystery Award. In addition
to the Spur Award–winning title novella, this volume also
contains stories featuring Bill Pronzini's famous "Nameless
Detective" and Marcia Muller's highly popular Sharon Mc-
Cone investigator.

ISBN 13: 978-0-8439-6341-0

A story so powerful that Clint Eastwood, who directed and starred in the 1976 film, has said it was his favorite movie to make.

The Outlaw Josey Wales

"A marathon chase that runs from Missouri to the Rio Grande, garnished with everything a Western outlaw could want. There are banks to rob, trusty sidekicks to ride with, blue-bellies to annihilate, and at the end of the trail a big surprise."
—*New York Times Book Review*

Josey Wales is out for blood. The Union Army slaughtered his family and lured his friends into a death trap under the guise of a white flag. The war may be over, but he refuses to surrender. No matter how far he has to ride, no matter how high the price on his head, no matter how much he hurts or hungers—he will get his vengeance.

Forrest Carter

ISBN 13: 978-0-8439-6346-5

Louis L'Amour

For millions of readers, the name Louis L'Amour is synonymous with the excitement of the Old West. His brilliant stories and novels capture all the adventure and action of those glorious days of the American frontier. But for too long, many of these tales have only been available in revised, altered versions, often very different from their original form. Here, collected together in paperback for the first time, are eight of L'Amour's finest stories, all carefully restored to their initial magazine publication versions.

These are stories of range wars and wagon trains, saloon singers and hired guns. They are tales of courage and danger, hardship and survival. And each thrilling story is presented the way Louis L'Amour originally wrote it, packed with the flavor and feel of the American West.

WEST OF THE TULAROSA

ISBN 13: 978-0-8439-6410-.

☐ **YES!**

ign me up for the Leisure Western Book Club and send
y FREE BOOKS! If I choose to stay in the club, I will pay
only $14.00* each month, a savings of $9.96!

AME: _____

DDRESS: _____

ELEPHONE: _____

MAIL: _____

☐ I want to pay by credit card.

☐ **VISA**   ☐ **MasterCard**   ☐ **DISCOVER**

CCOUNT #: _____

KPIRATION DATE: _____

GNATURE: _____

Mail this page along with $2.00 shipping and handling to:
Leisure Western Book Club
PO Box 6640
Wayne, PA 19087
Or fax (must include credit card information) to:
610-995-9274
You can also sign up online at **www.dorchesterpub.com**.
*Plus $2.00 for shipping. Offer open to residents of the U.S. and Canada only.
Canadian residents please call 1-800-481-9191 for pricing information.
under 18, a parent or guardian must sign. Terms, prices and conditions subject to
ange. Subscription subject to acceptance. Dorchester Publishing reserves the right
to reject any order or cancel any subscription.